CW00758527

Father, Forgive Me

Rebel Priest and Teenager in Death Tryst, the headline read.

The evidence seemed to bear out that a double suicide had actually occurred, but when an appeal for help brought ex-Detective Chief Superintendent Harry Bassett on to the scene his friends Inspector Bob Greenaway and Sergeant Andy Miller weren't complaining. Once they put their three heads together, the evidence soon began to look flimsy.

Who was the dead girl's mystery boyfriend whom she claimed she could never marry, if he was not the priest? Who was the father of her unborn child? Were they one and the same?

Bassett uncovers the tale of a love that is anything but life-enhancing and pits his wits against a clever murderer, who isn't quite clever enough.

by the same author

BURY HIM KINDLY
WREATH OF HONESTY
SCREAMING BONES

PAT BURDEN

Father, Forgive Me

THE CRIME CLUB
An Imprint of HarperCollins *Publishers*

In loving memory of Stuart

First published in Great Britain in 1993
by The Crime Club, an imprint of
HarperCollins Publishers, 77–85 Fulham Palace Road,
Hammersmith, London W6 8JB

9 8 7 6 5 4 3 2 1

A catalogue record for this book is
available from the British Library.

ISBN 0 00 232382 6

Photoset in Linotron Baskerville by
Rowland Phototypesetting Ltd
Bury St Edmunds, Suffolk
Printed and bound in Great Britain by
HarperCollins Book Manufacturing, Glasgow.

CHAPTER 1

When Bassett overheard the words 'Priest and a Slip of a Girl' spoken in the hushed half-malicious, half-gleeful tones of a gossip, he felt sorry for the hapless cleric, whoever he was, poor man. Probably the victim of his own innocence, spotted in what gossips of a certain kind might choose to call 'suspicious circumstances'.

It was one o'clock on a sunny if cool September day. Bassett sat alone at a table for two in the garden of the Pheasant, Oakleigh's village pub. After the *No Drink If You Drive* campaign had threatened his livelihood the pub's landlord, Archie Wood, had started to serve bar meals, and Bassett had taken to ambling along once or twice a week to 'partake'. He had finished eating, a Ploughman's today, and had been thinking idly that the cheese, pickle and hot crusty rolls had been so delicious he wished he had them to savour all over again, when the voice from the next table impinged upon his thoughts.

The 'Slip of a Girl' did it. 'Priest and a Girl' might have washed over him: just a re-hashing of another kiss and tell story. One of a flood since an unfortunate Bishop had confessed to being the father of a teenage son. But 'Slip of a Girl' smacked of embellishment, of malevolence even.

His mind continued to idle as he drank beer, filled his pipe. One advantage of eating outdoors: he could enjoy a smoke without feeling guilty. He felt a glow of contentment. A good meal, a smoke . . . He looked around lazily. Sunshine, fresh air, rolling countryside, a picturesque view of a black-and-white cottage, apples reddening on trees in an orchard—what more could a man want?

His smile became a sigh. He would have liked to have his dear Mary sitting opposite him.

It wasn't as if priests who fell in love and longed to marry were anything new, he was thinking, having stolen a look at the next table, when his ears pricked up again.

'. . . Not much more than a teenager. Had a flat at the Pugh-Talbots', nursed the old lady . . . You know it. Briony House. The big white house on the rise just before you get to the Glevebourne main road . . .'

A *local* affair?

Another quick look. The speaker was thirtyish, face pink with excitement, and no doubt the satisfaction of being the one to pass on the news. Companion prettier, pale, her mouth hanging open. 'I don't believe it!'

'It's true. There they were, together, holding hands. Dead, both of them . . . Knife, they say . . .'

Bassett concentrated on his pipe.

'Suicide pact, they're saying . . . I always said he was too good-looking to be a priest . . .'

Now the other joined in, a trifle reluctantly, but agreeing nevertheless. 'He *is* handsome. Was handsome, I should say. I only met him twice; once at the almshouses, I was visiting and so was he; once at Carnival time, when we were dressing a float. I did wonder why someone like him, so manly, had become a priest. A girl broke his heart, made him give up women, I thought. But suicide . . .' Came a gasp, and, 'I thought Catholics believed that those who committed suicide went straight to hell. Worse for a *priest* . . .'

'Well, that's what they're saying. There they were, lying by the car, hands touching . . .'

'Ohh . . . What did you say his name was? I only knew him by sight.'

'Lambert. Father Roger Lambert.'

'From St Chad's?'

'Yes.'

'He is the one I'm thinking of, then.'

A moment, and Bassett rose, gathered his empty plates and tankard on to a tray, and met genial landlord Archie at the bar door on his way out. 'Thought I'd save your legs, Archie!'

They both moved to one side to allow a customer, all perfume, smiles and clanking bracelets, to enter. 'Spare a minute? The two women at the table next to mine, Archie—do you know them?'

The landlord glanced across. 'The one wearing the pink Bermuda shorts and peaked cap is Gill Thomas. Lives in that converted barn behind the old rectory.'

'The other?'

'Darned if I can remember her name, only see her once in a blue moon. But an aunt of hers, Dolly Blest, used to live round here. Moved to Glevebourne a couple of years ago after her husband retired from Smith's farm. Good cook, the aunt. Could have done with her help, but six miles is a bit far for her to come. All right in summer, but in winter . . .'

'Does she by any chance cook for the Pugh-Talbots?'

'Matter of fact she does. 'Nother reason she turned me down; she was already fixed up—at the Pugh-Whatsits' and a Major Hay's. Last time I saw her, anyway. Why? You thinking of employing her yourself?'

Bassett returned the amused grin. 'What! When I can come here and eat like royalty!' No, he was simply thinking that if Dolly Blest did work for the Pugh-Whatsits this could explain the niece's apparent first-hand knowledge about a slip of a girl who lived there.

He rattled the tray of empty dishes. 'Best dispose of this. Grand lunch!' He took a step, paused. 'Seen Willy lately, Archie?'

Meaning Reverend William Brewerton, Vicar of Oakleigh, known to friends as Reverend Willy or just plain Willy.

'Not for several days.'

There was a gleam in Archie's eyes. Bassett sensed the question taking shape: What's it all about, Harry?

But Dolly Blest's niece and her friend Gill Thomas were on the move. 'I think they're going,' Archie observed. Bassett followed his gaze. 'I'd best make tracks myself.'

Had Archie voiced the question Bassett would have been loath to answer. For what did he know? Merely what he had overheard: a conversation between two women, one of whom might be a pathological liar or a joker of the far from pleasant kind. Certainly the niece had been laughing when she rose from the table, and Gill Thomas had seemed—well, she had looked as if she didn't know whether to laugh or to cry. As anyone might look who had been at the butt end of a bad joke.

On the other hand . . .

Old habits die hard. For all that Bassett would growl 'Retired!' when addressed as Detective Chief Superintendent Harry Bassett, he did occasionally don his copper's hat. He donned it now. Ambling home via leafy lanes, he mulled over what he had overheard.

Two items caused him concern. First, there was something odd about the suicide scene as described. A knife had been mentioned. A knife? Would a priest and a girl not much more than a teenager use a knife on themselves? Or each other? *There they were, lying by the car.* Why not use the car? A more peaceful end. Handful of tablets, painkillers, a hose, exhaust fumes, and sleep before oblivion, if die you must. Made far better sense.

If indeed the niece wasn't a liar.

She had spoken one truth, however. It was this second item that was uppermost in Bassett's mind, as, arrived home, he made himself a mug of coffee. There *was* a young

Father Lambert at St Chad's. Bassett had never met him, but Willy Brewerton had. Anglican Reverend Brewerton was a regular visitor to the presbytery: the incumbent there, Father Mike Fitzroy, was one of Willy's closest friends.

So, instead of mowing his lawn and picking damsons for his favourite jam, Bassett lazed the afternoon away, remaining within constant earshot of the telephone.

The call came. 'Harry? Willy Brewerton here. Are you free this evening? Could we talk?'

CHAPTER 2

Shortly before ten o'clock the following morning Bassett arrived at his local police station in the small market town of Glevebourne in Herefordshire.

He parked automatically in the Chief Super's spot, admired the tree-lined car park, leaves already taking on the pinks and golds of autumn, glanced up at Inspector Bob Greenaway's office window, and opened the boot of his old and much respected Citroën. He hauled out two bulging carrier bags.

About then, Andy Miller, Bob's sergeant, looked out of the window in passing, and halted, edging forward to see better. 'Bob—Bassett's coming.'

'Bassett?' Miles away.

'Best tweeds. New hat too by the looks of it.' Hats were the bane of Bassett's life, he was forever losing them.

'Remember the hippos dancing in that film, *Fantasia*? It's him,' Andy chuckled. 'Dancing on the steps with our WPC Mitchell. He tried to be gentlemanly and raise his hat, and missed. Arms full of carrier bags. Oops!'

'What?' Bob Greenaway was preoccupied with paperwork. 'Hippo? Has he put on weight?'

'No, guv.' Andy groaned. Bob was slow when he wanted to be. 'It was the dance—' Oh never mind. 'He's made a conquest. You should see how Mitchell is smiling at him!'

At last it registered. 'Bassett?' Bob looked up. And sank back heavily into his chair. 'I wonder what he wants,' he said tonelessly.

'Probably just a social call, guv. Been ages since we saw him. And there's apples in them thar bags. One collapsed. Mitchell's helping him pick them up.'

'Beware a Bassett bearing gifts,' Bob said morosely.

A short silence fell.

Andy turned to face his gaffer. Their eyes locked. 'You thinking what I'm thinking, guv?'

'When did we have a murder case, Andy, that Bassett didn't show up for?'

'Officially it's not murder.'

''Tis now. I'll bet on it.' Bob showed the whites of his eyes. 'Andy—I'm going to broach the subject anyway. But I'll do it my way. You let on and I'll cancel your next leave. Crikey!' He shot a look towards the door. 'He's quick on his pins this morning!' He began gesturing frantically, as if Andy had been deaf to the exchanges of 'Good Morning!' outside in the corridor.

When Bassett's rap on wood was followed by his head poking round the door, Bob was immersed in a pile of papers, Andy searching through a filing cabinet.

Andy turned. 'Look who's here! 'Morning, guvnor.' He grinned, stared overtly at Bassett's empty hands and went into his act. 'Loves Worcester Pearmains, my ma,' he moaned. 'Kill for a bag, she would. Never thought we'd have a pal with an orchard overflowing with 'em who wouldn't bring us a few—'

Bassett grinned at the performance and tossed his car keys. 'Box each in the boot. No virtue in my lugging them up here for you to have to lug them down again. Left the others at Reception for sharing out.'

Andy gone, Bob waved Bassett to a chair. 'Take a pew.'

Bassett did so. 'You look fit, Robert.' Still lean, pin neat. Would look distinguished when the black hair had finished turning grey.

'You look disgustingly healthy yourself. Full of the joys of autumn. Still got your dog?'

'She's on holiday.'

'You're pulling my leg, of course.'

'Don't know that I am,' Bassett chuckled. 'She is keeping a recently widowed neighbour company.'

'I thought you were inseparable.'

'We are. I take her for romps morning and evening. It's only for a few days, until my neighbour goes to live with her daughter. She's been burgled twice. A dog on the premises—'

'Is an excellent burglar alarm,' Bob finished for him. He treated Bassett to a rare smile. 'My wife will be glad of the apples. Thanks.'

'You're welcome.' Bassett tipped his hat to the back of his head. 'Time for a chat?'

'About a priest and a girl? . . . The only deaths we're investigating,' Bob said, in response to raised eyebrows.

'Might as well come straight to the point, then, eh? Remember Reverend William Brewerton? The Wilson murder?'

'The body of Derek Wilson was found in his churchyard.'

'Willy Brewerton came to see me last night. He's a close friend of Father Mike Fitzroy, who doesn't accept a suicide finding. As I think you already know.'

'What does Reverend Brewerton think took place?'

'He wants me to find out. No offence to you. He came to me as a friend.'

'Have you spoken to Father Fitzroy?'

'No, I decided to come to you first.'

'Facts being more useful then sentiment.' Bob nodded. Nearly smiled again, twice in one day. 'To begin with, the suicide pact is a theory. Secondly, between you and me, it is giving me a headache.' He reached for a file. 'Facts. We'll start with the girl.

'Shirley Hughes. Nineteen, nearly twenty. Father not known. Mother dumped her in an orphanage when she was three. Fostered out. Nice kid, by all accounts, except for a superior attitude, believed herself a cut above some of those she came into contact with, including some of the foster parents—'

'May I interrupt, Bob? *Some* of the foster parents? She had several?'

'From twelve onwards, yes. Because of her attitude. Considered a bad influence on younger children.'

'Airs and graces?'

'That's about the size of it. Nothing more serious,' Bob said. 'At sixteen she started applying for live-in jobs. She had found out that with proper consent there was nothing to stop her striking out for independence. She was lucky. She landed a job at a girls' public school, assistant to the matron.

'There she met Father Lambert. He used to visit a young relative whose parents were abroad, attached to the diplomatic service. According to Father Fitzroy, Shirley approached Father Lambert: someone to talk to who had no axe to grind. He saw her regularly after that, helped her find holiday jobs, and when she was eighteen recommended her to Mrs Pugh-Talbot. Mrs Pugh-T's mother was terminally ill, they had a day nurse, required a night nurse. Shirley got the job, which lasted for nearly a year. She was at the school, Oakdean, for nigh on two years.

'The old lady died, the day nurse moved on, Shirley stayed, in the flat the day nurse vacated. Mrs Pugh-T had a high opinion of her, she had nowhere else to go, and in any event the arrangement was temporary; Shirley was aiming to do a nursing course eventually. Meanwhile she worked as a Carer. Casual work, in private homes, nursing homes and hospital. Successfully, apparently. She was able to pay her way . . . You know the Pugh-Talbots?'

'A well-known local family, Willy told me.'

'Not as prominent as they were,' Bob Greenaway said. 'Still one of Glevebourne's top families, though. Mrs Pugh-T gave the girl a good name, says she was clean-living, kind to her mother, conscientious, capable and honest.

'Now Father Lambert. Young, modern, energetic, hard worker for the community. Nice chap all round, seemingly. Nobody interviewed to date admits to hearing anything in the gossip line about him or the girl. Most refused even to think any bad about him. One or two hemmed and hawed and reminded us he was an advocate of priests being allowed to marry, and one or two went so far as to say: Well, he was good-looking. But they were strictly after-the-event views in my opinion. If he were still alive I doubt that any thought of an entanglement would have entered their heads. Incidentally, we've kept questions low-profile, so to speak. Did anyone know of any reason why Father Lambert and the girl should be together at that particular spot? That kind of question.

'Now to events leading up to their deaths,' Bob continued. 'Reverend Brewerton told you she was pregnant?'

'Yes.'

'Right. On Tuesday last week Shirley took four-year-old twins to dancing class. Neighbour of the Pugh-Talbots. Their nanny sick, Shirley filling the breach. Nanny used to stay at the studio and watch, Shirley did not. She went to see Father Lambert, spent twenty minutes with him. Three days later, same thing: dropped the twins off, asked the dance teacher to be sure they waited for her, and went.

'We know she went to the doctor's, from there, again, to the presbytery. The assumption is that on Tuesday she told the priest what she suspected, on Friday it had been confirmed by the doctor—that she was expecting.

'After leaving the presbytery she collected the twins, took them home, and stayed until around four-thirty, when their mother got in from work. Mother's a lawyer.

'Shirley was seen returning to her flat shortly after five p.m. by Mrs Pugh-Talbot, the cook, and a gardener.

'The entrance to the flat is at the side of the house. Inside the house there's an access door to the flat leading from a corridor to the old nursery suite, which had been converted to bedroom, sitting-room etcetera for Mrs P-T's mother. The door has bolts both sides, a hangover from the days of the nanny, who liked her privacy when off duty.

'At five-thirty Mrs Pugh-Talbot went to see Shirley. She's a businesswoman, fashion shops, and wanted the girl to assist with a show she was putting on for the Children in Need charity. She went via the access door, which was then unbolted. Found the girl in bed with a headache.

'At six-thirty she went again. This time the access door was bolted. However, she heard sounds of drawers being opened and shut, and assumed Shirley was getting ready to go out.

'At seven-fifteen p.m. she saw Shirley and the priest leaving in his car. An elderly relative, known affectionately as Uncle Bertie, was in the drive coming back from taking the dogs for a walk. He also saw them. In fact the car had very nearly knocked him down. And so far as we've been able to discover, that was the last anyone saw of them alive.

'The car and their bodies were found on Saturday afternoon by two women blackberry picking. Doc McPherson says they had been dead for between eighteen and twenty hours, which would seem to indicate that they went directly to the beauty spot.'

Bob added: 'We haven't released information about the pregnancy. Hardly necessary,' he said acidly. 'Some folk appear to have decided it for themselves.'

He paused. 'Something else we're sitting on. Father Lambert was stabbed, a swift clean blow to the heart—but the girl was strangled.'

CHAPTER 3

Bassett was speechless for a moment. Then: 'Hardly suicide, is it?'

'In the girl's case, no, not in my book. But there is a theory . . .' Bob Greenaway hesitated. 'The theory is that there was a suicide pact originally; but the man was a priest, a carer of souls, the soul more important than a body. Oh, the dickens with it, Harry,' he continued in a rush. 'The theory is that the priest decided that the girl must not kill herself.'

'Therefore he strangled her?' Bassett took a breath. 'Bizarre.' He shuddered, said sharply, 'Whose theory?'

'Monsignor sent by the Bishop. It's just feasible. The girl appears to have done little to defend herself, in fact seems to have been a willing victim.'

'Right-oh.' Who was Bassett to argue with Catholic officials? Yet. 'The Priest and the girl drive to a beauty spot, where he strangles the girl—'

Bob shook his head. 'She might have been strangled in bed. Traces of bed fluff and soap powder dust under her fingernails. Could be she did struggle—she'd have to, wouldn't she, for heaven's sake!—but was pinned beneath the sheets. Also, she had tea with the twins. We can't be positive, but stomach contents . . . Jim McPherson thinks she could have died anything up to an hour before the priest.'

Bassett stared. 'He strangles her, dresses her—I take it she was dressed? All right, he finishes dressing her. Carries her out to his car . . .' His face fell apart.

Bob Greenaway agreed with a look. 'But all part of a plan, Harry. They had to be found together.'

'They left no letter?'

'No need. The story was there, told in full by their bodies lying by the car.'

'Another theory?'

'Same one. The Church is ready to accept that Father Lambert fell prey to his own liberal attitudes, simultaneously battled with his conscience about sleeping with the girl, and when she fell pregnant his already tormented mind gave way completely.'

'The girl's too, I suppose,' Bassett growled. 'Or do they point out that she was at an impressionable age?' He glared at Bob Greenaway. 'They want to see the back of it, I imagine? Discretion the keynote.'

Affirmed.

'You?' Bassett said.

'We've given it everything we've got and all we've come up with so far seems to bear out that what appears to have happened did happen. Had the girl been molested, or the knife used on her, we could have considered a mugging or sexual attack, the priest hurrying to her rescue. But the fact that she was strangled, that she and the priest were seen leaving together, the time element, plus one or two additional items . . .'

He didn't finish. His eyes said it all.

And if Bassett read him correctly, Bob was begging.

Bassett tapped his notebook. 'Could we clarify one or

two points before I forget them? You say three people saw the girl at five p.m.'

'Yes. They were in the garden. Mrs Pugh-Talbot hadn't long got home herself. She and the gardener, a Tom Johnson, were discussing flowers for a dinner-party Mrs P-T had the next day. The cook, a Mrs Blest, was about to leave. She lives in town, cooks as required.'

'That was five p.m. Mrs Pugh-T and a relative saw Father Lambert's car driving away at seven-fifteen. Did no one see him arrive?'

'Apparently not. After the cook and gardener knocked off Mrs Pugh-Talbot was alone. She thinks the priest must have arrived while she was in the kitchen.'

'Which presumably is at the back of the house. The entrance to the girl's flat—?'

'At the front. Side of the house, to be exact. Big house, set in a small country estate. Long drive from the road, no close neighbours. Small lodge half way along the main drive, but the tenants were out on Friday evening.'

'Where was Mrs Pugh-T when she saw Shirley leaving?'

'Front of the house,' Bob said. 'Drawing-room.'

'Drawing-room,' Bassett said thoughtfully. 'A long drive up to a big house. Country estate. Implies space. Reason tells me the car was unlikely to pass *close* to the drawing-room window. Daylight fading at that hour. It usually seems darker anyhow when you are indoors looking out . . .'

Which did Mrs Pugh-Talbot recognize? he asked himself. The car or Father Lambert?

'These additional items, Bob—'

Bob Greenaway had them listed.

1. Father Lambert was a staunch supporter of certain reforms, priests being allowed to marry, for instance.
2. He was aware of his attractiveness to certain women.

Was inclined to joke about it. That he was sufficiently aware has been interpreted by some as a sign of weakness; if he were truly steadfast he would have been blissfully *un*aware.

3. In retrospect he did appear to see rather too much of the girl, and be too concerned about her welfare.
4. Shirley told friends she had a boyfriend, but *could never marry him*.
5. When she first suspected she was pregnant she told the maid-of-all work at the Pugh-Talbot house that it was a terrible mistake. *And*: She refused to name the man responsible; she couldn't, she said, because if word got round *he would lose everything*. (Maid's name is Helen Fletcher.)

'*He* would lose everything?' Bassett said. 'She was concerned for *him*, not for herself?'

'You see the difficulty, Harry. Suggests the priest.'

'Or the boyfriend. Any advance on him?'

None. Blanks. 'Shirley kept his identity secret.'

'Ergo the unnamed father of the child and the elusive boyfriend could be one and the same.'

They could. 'Could be the priest,' said Bob.

'I could argue some of those items you've listed—'

'So could I, Harry.' Bob shrugged. 'In fact I have. But I come unstuck on one that isn't listed—the knife. It came from Shirley's flat. Mrs Pugh-Talbot saw it on a table in the kitchen at five-thirty. How did it get to the scene of the crime unless the priest or Shirley took it with them?'

Bassett nodded. 'Good point. The three who saw the girl at five o'clock—I imagine it was her car they saw. Would that have been from a distance?'

'Could she have had a passenger? We thought of that. Answer's no. The cook went and spoke to her. She was all alone.'

'Alone in the car. Alone in the flat at five-thirty, until Mrs Pugh-T got there. Alone at six-thirty, getting ready to go out. Or was she? Mrs Pugh-T only *heard* Shirley at six-thirty. More accurately, heard sounds she thought were made by drawers being opened and shut. Didn't see Shirley. Didn't *see* her between five-thirty and seven-fifteen. Two hours. Moreover, Mrs Pugh-T was also alone . . . Mmm. This other witness to them leaving. A relative? A member of the family?'

'Uncle Bertie.' Bob narrowed his eyes. 'What's on your mind? I can see your cogs working.'

'The girl was expecting a baby. Fact. If it wasn't the priest's, whose was it? I am informed there is a son. There is also Mrs Pugh-Talbot's husband; and Uncle Bertie.'

Bob flicked through a clutch of papers, found the one he sought. 'Bertie lives in the village, an estate cottage. Takes the house dogs for walks most days. Last Friday he left the big house at four p.m., returned at seven-fifteen.'

'Three hours?' Bassett said dubiously.

It checked out, Bob said. 'He called on an old lady, an old retainer who loves dogs. Her own died, unfair of her to have another at her age, so on fine-weather days he takes the house dogs on a visit.'

'Any particular day? Every Monday? Tuesday?'

'As he tells it, they go when fancy dictates, weather permitting.'

'So. Friday was a nice day. So was Thursday. Also Wednesday, if memory serves.' Thoughtful eyes met Bob's across the desk. 'How good is the old retainer's memory? What is he like, Uncle Bertie?'

'Bit of a character. Seems a decent chap, though.'

Decent enough to lie to help a member of his family?

Not worth saying aloud. Ask another.

'Willy Brewerton said something about the son and Mr Pugh-Talbot not getting home till eight o'clock.'

'Correct,' said Bob Greenaway. 'Mr works in London, comes home for weekends. Got home on Friday at his usual time, roughly eight. The son, Julian, stopped off en route from Oxford to his girlfriend's home, Westonby Park, again at eight.' Bob spread his hands. 'Father and son nowhere in the vicinity at seven-fifteen. They also check out.'

Bassett paused for more thought, then crooked a finger and peered at the files on Bob Greenaway's desk. 'May I have a peak at the photographs?'

They were handed to him. 'Know what annoys me most about this?' Bob said. 'We haven't a clue as to how the suicide theory got started. But it's impeded us at every turn.'

'So, I fancy, has the religious aspect.'

Bassett watched the other try not to nod. 'Difficult, I agree.' He studied the pile of photographs, some longer than the main pile. When at length he spoke again, it was with some bewilderment. 'From what Willy said—' (and his own bit of eavesdropping)— 'I imagined the scene itself gave rise to the suicide pact theory. Bloodstained lovers holding hands. But these . . .'

He picked up a print. 'The girl fully dressed, lying semi-prone on the ground, one arm outstretched. But the man is only reaching for the girl, he's barely touching her. And the drag marks on the grass—he's obviously dragged himself a distance, he was nowhere near her when he died. Not what I would call a clear-cut suicide pact scene.'

'Especially since one of the bodies is unmistakably that of a priest,' Bob Greenaway agreed. 'His black robe was on the back seat of the car, but he's wearing other vestments.'

'So how come?'

'A catalogue of—! I won't say it, Harry. Start with the woman who phoned in. She was virtually incoherent. The message that got across was a garbled account of a car and two people nearby who might be dead. Uniformed branch took it to be a traffic accident, and proceeded accordingly.

'As they tell it, a small crowd had gathered by the time they got there, whispers already circulating—Suicide pact. God knows who started it. A WPC inquired in vain. None of the sightseers was keen to stay and answer questions, and in an area like that there wasn't a cat in hell's chance of detaining them. You're with me so far?

'When we got there the crowd had dispersed, leaving the two women who found the bodies and a cocky cub reporter falling over himself with enthusiasm. Was he the lucky one! What a story! And him on the spot! A scoop! And he'd only been a reporter for ten months! Even wanted our names, Andy's and mine, so as to give us a good write-up! Turned out he worked on the *Gazette*. I metaphorically boxed his ears and sent him packing.

'Sunday morning his editor comes here, one of Father Lambert's flock, so his interest was personal as well as professional. Apparently the cub reporter had been to his house with a draft of his "scoop". He couldn't fault the youth's keenness, what worried him was the content. Choice of two headlines: "Rebel Priest and Teenager in Death Tryst" was one; the other: "The Secret Torment of a young Catholic Priest". Followed by a piece that was sympathetically done, credit where due: a story-book tale of hopeless love.'

Bassett's eyes rounded to match Bob Greenaway's. 'As you say, keen. Anyone ask him where his imaginative ideas came from?'

'The evidence that was there for all to see, was his explanation. Plus snippets gleaned from comments made by the crowd, one of whom identified the girl, said she was nineteen and a good friend of Father Lambert's.'

'A faceless informer,' Bassett muttered. 'Did he say how he happened to be on the spot?'

'He'd heard how a farmer was beating the drought, was on his way for a look-see.'

'And came upon something better. I'll buy that,' Bassett said. 'I gather you nipped his "scoop" in the bud. What resurrected the suicide theory?'

'You may well ask. He phoned Father Fitzroy—for an interview. Shambles there too. Father Fitzroy immediately contacted his superiors; we know with what result. Father Fitzroy has since regretted acting so hastily. At the time, he says, his intention was to have someone from a higher authority at his side when the story broke.'

'A story he neglected to verify first.'

Bob Greenaway picked up photographs at random. 'I've aired my doubts, they've all been explained away by those who want to settle for the suicide pact theory . . .'

'They are?' Bassett said.

'Why did the priest take the girl's body out of the car? Why did he get out? He could as easily have knifed himself in his seat. Why go to the picnic spot? Why not stay at the flat? Why leave everything open-ended? Why no Confession? I'm no Catholic but I've always understood that Confession was central to the Faith—'

The telephone rang. The call was brief. 'The Chief.'

Bassett made as if to rise. Bob waved him down. 'No need to go. The files are there. Just remember to fib a bit if you're caught snooping.'

Seconds later, alone, Bassett was murmuring: 'And why was the priest's black cassock folded up on the back seat?'

Was it bloodstained? He checked the notes: It wasn't. Nor was there any knife damage. Father Lambert hadn't been wearing it when he died.

CHAPTER 4

Sergeant Andy Miller returned to the office first. 'I hear you're with us, guvnor.'

Bassett received his car keys. 'On the case?' A nod, a wink, a finger to his lips, and 'Ssh . . .'

Andy beamed. 'I got held up. What have I missed?'

Bassett brought him up to date. 'Time for a chat?' he said then.

Andy grabbed a chair. 'Found something?'

'No glaring discrepancy—'

'Pity.' As he sat next to Bassett, and grinned.

'I've heard the pet theory about why the priest might have strangled Shirley, Andy. Any others? Hinted at during questioning. Or among yourselves?'

'Only related to his flipping his lid. If he did,' Andy replied. 'On Friday morning Shirley said something about abortion, on Friday evening he went to talk her out of it, when he failed he lost his cool. Overlooking that by killing Shirley he destroyed the child as well. *That* was the reason he took his own life.'

'Your answer to that?'

'Priests don't lose their cool. It's against all their natural inclinations. And training—all those years in a seminary. Besides, he couldn't have tried coaxing her for long.'

'On Friday night, no. We don't know, however, what passed between them in the morning. Maybe she already had a clinic booked. Maybe the assault began as a physical attempt to stop her. If she had her coat on—'

'We think she was strangled in bed.'

'Might have got in fully dressed when she heard him coming.'

'No suitcase packed, guvnor.'

'He might have unpacked it.' But neither of them truly thought so. 'You're right. Why would he bother?' Bassett motioned. 'Carry on.'

Scarcely worth a mention, Andy said, but as it had been suggested—'She might have tried to blackmail him. He couldn't stomach the gossip—'

'So there was gossip?' Bassett said with a sidelong look.

'Sorry, guvnor, I should have said fear of gossip. Say she wanted him to give up the priesthood and threatened to expose him if he wouldn't.'

'Wouldn't have had much to gain, would she? On the other hand—' Bassett's voice tautened—'as a theory it isn't bad—if you forget the priest and think of threats directed at someone else.'

The real father of the child, for instance.

'What's your theory, Andy?'

'Same as yours, guvnor, whatever it is,' the sergeant replied with a grin. 'You know me, I stick with the smart money.'

Bassett laughed and began filling his pipe.

'Let's take gossip for a minute,' he said slowly; 'or to put it crudely, folk who run off at the mouth. A double suicide had already been decided upon when you and Bob got to the scene. What would it take to start the idea? A whisper: Looks as if they've killed themselves. Another: I always knew no good would come of it. Follow with: Pregnant. Which is an even juicier titbit. Guaranteed to have ears stretching six feet high. Then: I knew her. Ah-ha! That does it. One person dodging about could have done all the whispering up to then. Now other minds come into play. Knew her . . . knew the girl . . . must have known what was going on . . . Perhaps they have killed themselves . . . If the girl is pregnant . . .

'Suddenly it's all true! The crowd believe it; enough of

them to matter. Whoever started the whispering knows he or she has succeeded; can slip away. *The priest and Shirley Hughes are inextricably linked.*'

'You think it was deliberate?' Andy said soberly.

Bassett looked at him. 'Be interesting to find out.'

He had filled his pipe, gazed round while patting his pockets for his lighter. 'Can't smoke in here, can I? Not to worry.' He heaved himself to his feet. 'The car here?'

'In the pound.' Andy was collecting the files to lock them away. 'I'll come with you.'

On the way there Bassett asked: 'This eager-beaver reporter: did he have a camera with him?'

The car, a blue Ford Escort, was isolated in a taped-off area of the covered pound.

'Forensic have done with it,' Andy said. 'Father Lambert's cassock, hat and bag of tricks were on the back seat. Ballpoint, car manual and the usual scrap paper in the glove box. Driving gloves, a torch, one of those heavy rubber-coated ones, on the front seat. That's about it.'

'Forensic got hat, torch, dirt off the pedals?'

'They went by the book, guvnor.'

Bob Greenaway joined them, looking pleased with himself. 'I've managed to convince the gaffer that we need more time, Shirley's so-called boyfriend must be identified even if he turns out to be the priest. She must have told somebody who he was. I'm off to say hello to various foster parents and the school where she worked. Might take a good couple of days.'

Andy?

'Resources don't run to expenses for two,' Bob informed his sergeant; adding drily, 'I knew you'd be heartbroken,' when he intercepted Andy's grin. 'As for you, Harry—'

'Mmm?' Bassett said, straight-faced.

'I think the gaffer's wise to us, meaning you. Has been for some time.'

'Slipped up, eh?' He turned to Andy. 'Might account for them dragging their feet over your promotion, lad. We'll be sneaky with this one.'

'Starting tomorrow,' Bob Greenaway advised. 'At this minute you're the illegitimate pointy-head who pinched his car space this morning.'

They watched him go. 'Where do we start, guvnor?'

'From scratch, Andy.' Bassett liked the young copper; reminded him of himself many moons ago. 'And we get tough. No more pussy-footing. Forget suicide. Forget the man was a priest. From now on as far as you and I are concerned he is a victim, and we are investigating murder. Right?'

'Right.'

'Here's what we do . . .' They walked shoulder to shoulder away from the pound.

CHAPTER 5

Modest St Chad's and its adjoining presbytery was built in the middle of the nineteenth century, after Catholics in England achieved full civil rights, in what was then a quiet lane on the edge of Glevebourne. That once quiet lane was now, by small-town standards, a busy thoroughfare; and to harmonize with modern buildings grown up around it the church environs had been given a face-lift. Gone were the iron railings and wooden gates . . .

The presbytery, however, seemed little changed. It had all the right smells: old wood lovingly preserved with beeswax, old leather-bound books . . . and the scent of old-fashioned roses wafting in through the windows of the study into which Bassett was shown.

'Father Fitzroy will be so very pleased to see you. Terrible, isn't it? Terrible! Do help yourself to a sherry, he'll be with you directly.'

Mrs Pomfrey, the housekeeper, reminded Bassett of a childhood aunt. Same round, kind face; dimpled elbows; and mode of dress. He had never seen Aunt Charlotte in any colour but grey or navy blue, yet could never recall her looking dowdy. A gentle soul.

Mrs Pomfrey might simply be in mourning, of course.

Thus Bassett kept his voice and the warmth of smile down, as befitted a house of bereavement, when he said, 'I should appreciate a few words with you, Mrs Pomfrey, before I go.'

'I'll be here,' she said.

Father Mike Fitzroy was stocky and white-haired. He had the makings of a strong masculine face but somewhere along the line a weakness and over-softness had crept in.

'Good of you to come.' His handshake lacked firmness, but his voice was attractive, brushed as it was with a hint of the Irish. 'I've been at a loss to know what to do.'

'I can reassure you on one point, Father. Our police are continuing to investigate.'

'Are they now?' Pale grey eyes changed to blue. 'Oh, sure and that's a relief.' A square pale hand motioned. 'A glass of sherry? Not too early for you?'

Bassett watched the priest so gracefully to the drinks tray on a side table. 'Shirley and Father Lambert had known each other how long, Father?'

'Three years, three and a half.'

'How often did he see her?'

'Quite often, they were friends.' He handed Bassett a generously filled glass. 'Shall we sit down?'

They both sat.

'It has been suggested that he was over-concerned about her welfare,' Bassett said.

'No,' the elderly priest said vigorously. 'He greatly admired and respected Shirley. So many young people in her position choose a downward path, whereas Shirley set herself upward targets, she was determined to prove her worth. There was a fondness, I admit,' he continued more slowly. 'Shirley was somehow special. But we all have our favourite people, those we love and admire a little better than others. Even priests.'

A pained expression crossed his face. 'You're thinking of my reaction to the young reporter's request for an interview? I didn't know the voice on the telephone belonged to a young man, he could have been any age. And he spoke with authority. He seemed to know what he was talking about—he'd just left the scene, the police were there in force—' His shoulders moved. 'All the same I should not have acted so precipitately, it was an unpardonable lack of judgement on my part.'

'Not unpardonable,' Bassett said kindly. 'He is, I am told, an exceptionally assertive youngster.' He sipped sherry and complimented Father Fitzroy on his choice. 'Would you tell me about Shirley's visits to Father Lambert last week?'

'Yes. I was not as forthcoming as I ought to have been with your colleagues, so much is open to misinterpretation. The truth is, Father Lambert was sorely troubled last week. After Shirley left on Tuesday he was uncommonly thoughtful. On Friday, while he was waiting for her, I found him staring out of a window, again deep in thought, and all he would say in reply to my solicitations was that he felt inadequate. A feeling I shared when I was unable to help him.'

'He asked for your help?'

'On the contrary. Although there wasn't really time,

because Shirley arrived. After she had gone he seemed more relaxed. Not completely, there was still something on his mind, but I thought the strain had been lifted. I guessed that a solution to Shirley's problem, whatever it was, had been glimpsed.'

'You knew nothing about the baby?'

'Not until Monday, when your colleagues informed me. I realized then the possible nature of the problem. Not, I hasten to add, that Roger Lambert was responsible, but that he was deeply concerned for her. Disappointed too, I would imagine, having held her in high esteem.'

'But he still didn't discuss it with you?'

'No. Do you see why I omitted to tell your colleagues?' the priest said sadly. 'We had an agreement not to interfere in one another's problems unless invited to do so, but would the police have believed me if I had told them that? . . . Roger would have confided in me eventually, I'm sure. He made the first move on Friday evening, there really hadn't been time, again, on Friday afternoon, since Mrs Pomfrey's daughter-in-law had brought her children for tea. Shall I go on?'

'Please do,' Bassett said.

'They were here most of the afternoon. We had tea at four, a jolly affair. At around five-thirty Mrs Pomfrey and I went with the family to their car, Roger waved them off from the doorway. When I came back in he was on the phone, presumably to Briony House, asking to be put through to Shirley. Then he turned to me and said, as if I knew all about it: "I'm going to have one last try before she goes." And something about not being convinced she was doing the right thing.

'He must have been told Shirley wasn't answering, I think she's on an extension, because he said: "She is in, though? Good. Excellent. I'm on my way."

'He put the receiver down, told me he was going out and

would go on to the Cottage Hospital and one or two other calls. His normal Friday evening routine.'

'How did he look? Worried?'

'No, hopeful. As if all was not lost.'

'What time was it when he left, Father?'

'The clock struck six as he went out the door.'

'And when did you notice he was missing?'

'The following morning, Saturday. He never skipped his breakfast. He would "stoke up" as he called it, to last him through the day if necessary. But on Saturday there was no sign of him. We waited an hour, thinking he might have been held over at the hospital or fetched to an emergency, although normally he would have got a message to us somehow, then at ten o'clock I started phoning round.'

'You contacted Briony House, naturally?'

A nod. 'They said he had left there at seven-fifteen the previous evening.'

'Now that you do know about the baby, and have had time to think, have you any ideas?' Bassett said. 'For example, about a solution that might have been glimpsed.'

Father Fitzroy had given it some thought, he said. He paused, pushing out his lips to form an O, frowned as he said slowly, 'There were obviously no wedding plans in the offing for Shirley. If I heard Father Lambert correctly, and I am sure I did, Shirley was going somewhere; he was going to have one last try at something before she went. What was Shirley going to do? Was she going away, on her own, to have the child? Was she proposing to shoulder everything herself, and seek no help from the father of her unborn child? It is the only explanation I can think of that would also explain Roger Lambert's attitude. If I'm right, well, he would not have approved, he held strong views on responsibility. He would have tried to get her to seek support from the man, whoever he was. To be honest, knowing

Roger Lambert, I'd have to say he would be firmly resolved to have the man honour entirely his obligations.

'I'll hazard a guess that on her first visit Shirley refused to name names. On her second—I wonder if she made a half-promise. Perhaps to do something about a paternity claim after she had left the area. In which case Roger might have gone to see her in the evening hoping to strengthen the argument he had already put forward.

'Or,' the priest said earnestly, 'he might even have gone to have one last try at finding out who the man was.' His look became drawn. 'Succeeded. And died for his pains.'

He regarded Bassett searchingly. 'I am only guessing,' he said at length, rising. 'Shall I fetch Mrs Pomfrey now?'

The housekeeper had been preparing lunch; she smelt cool: of cucumber.

She had Aunt Charlotte's shy smile.

'Shirley's visits last week, Mrs Pomfrey.' Bassett lowered his voice: 'I'm sure you won't mind what I'm going to say. You are a mother, a grandmother, I believe—and Shirley was, well, young, alone and in trouble. Did she say anything to you in confidence that you haven't felt able to pass on to the police or Father Fitzroy?'

'No. No, nothing like that.'

'What did she say?'

'Very little. She asked to see Father Lambert, rather urgently. This was on Tuesday.'

'How was she, tearful? Unhappy?'

'There was *some*thing wrong,' Mrs Pomfrey said. 'Now I know about the baby I could say she was putting a brave face on. But she didn't say anything about it to me, no.'

'And on Friday?'

'She looked tired. I remarked upon it, but she laughed it off. She had been looking after two boisterous four-year-olds all week, she said.'

'Now, again please don't be offended, but did you, when you took tea in, perhaps, hear any of what passed between Shirley and Father Lambert?'

Mrs Pomfrey gave a funny little nod. 'I did. I heard two words: This Weekend. Shirley said them, Father Lambert repeated them. And I'm quite sure they had no connection with—with what happened later, because of the *way* they said them. Quite straightforwardly. As if Father Lambert had asked a question and Shirley answered: This Weekend.'

'Mm. Something was going to take place at the weekend. Meaning last weekend.'

'Is it of any use to you?'

'Of considerable use, Mrs Pomfrey. Thank you.'

'Do you think she was going to tell *him*?'

'That she was expecting his baby? Possible, isn't it? If only we knew who he was.' Bassett sighed. 'No ideas? No mention of him, by profession or trade if not by name? In the past, a word or suggestion—?'

Alas, no, the housekeeper said. She and Father Fitzroy had been shocked to learn about the baby; it had never occurred to them that Shirley might have a young man. Shirley had never mentioned a boyfriend, nor had she or Father Lambert ever so much as hinted that there might be one.

'It's very sad, isn't it, Mr Bassett?'

'It is, Mrs Pomfrey.'

He smiled. 'You saw Father Lambert leave on Friday evening?'

'I saw him go into the church.'

'When was this?'

'He left the house as the clock was striking six. He always went to say a prayer before going visiting.'

'Part of his routine?'

'Oh yes. Five minutes in church before he went out. His

injection, he used to say. Not of faith, faith he had plenty of. An injection of strength, to help him deal with sickness and grief. I've seen him moved to tears often, in private. He was a good man.'

She was close to tears herself now. 'This young man of Shirley's,' she said. 'I think he must have appeared on the scene recently. If she had been courting him for any length of time she would have brought him to meet us, I'm sure. Or would at least have spoken about introducing him to us. I don't know. I just don't know. It's all very mysterious. I've even wondered if—well, she was an innocent, you know. I can't help wondering if some man took *advantage* of her.'

A more worthwhile visit than anticipated, Bassett told himself, departing. He reflected on what he had learnt. It still wasn't clear why Shirley had gone to see Father Lambert twice last week. If Father Fitzroy's guess was near the mark and Shirley planned to go away to have the baby, all she had needed to do was go once to say goodbye. Mm? Perhaps this had been her intention on Tuesday, but Father Lambert had refused to let it rest there.

What had changed by Friday? Had Shirley decided to meet the priest half way? 'I'll tell the baby's father . . . this weekend.' Was that it? Mrs Pomfrey thought it was. She had agreed to tell a boyfriend *she could never marry* that she was carrying his child? But remained obstinately against divulging his name to anyone else?

But it posed an essential question: Why could she never marry the man?

And another: Had Father Lambert gone for one last try to get his identity? And succeeded . . . ?

Bassett had halted twice during his deliberations; had barely reached his car when he heard Father Fitzroy's shout: 'Mr Bassett! Telephone!'

. . . 'Yes, Andy?'

'Works like a charm, your turning up, guvnor. Doc's been on. Father Lambert's post-mortem. Seems we're on the right track. The priest didn't top himself.

CHAPTER 6

'Loose tooth.' Silver-haired Jim McPherson, friend and pathologist, held out a kidney dish. 'Lower canine. Pre-molar next to it is still in its socket but wobbly. Corresponding broken skin inside the cheek is consistent, I'd say, with a sock on the jaw, which could well have knocked him out.'

'Meaning?'

'Throws doubt on suicide.'

Which was what they wanted to hear.

'Also this. Small cut on top of the head.' Doc eased aside some of the priest's black hair. 'I saw this on day one when I was checking for additional external injuries, but put it down to a bump he might have received when he fell.' He addressed Bassett and Andy with a single sweeping glance. 'Put the two injuries together—significant, I'd say.'

'A means of getting him into the car with a dead girl, and away to the beauty spot without protest,' Bassett said. 'Unconscious, he wouldn't have known what was going on till it was too late. Correct?'

'That's pretty well what I had in mind. He might have been hit twice.'

Bassett fingered the pipe in his pocket. 'Mind if I smoke?' It wasn't the slab, it was the smell of the place, the hospital smell, that caused him to feel fragile.

'Hot coffee in the pot.' Doc motioned, including Andy in the invitation. 'Have a read of my notes while you're at it.'

'We'd sooner you told us,' Bassett said. 'We'll not say no to the coffee, though, provided it's been nowhere near your chemicals.'

'No marks on the jaw, Andy,' he observed while Doc was scrubbing his hands. 'Bruising's inside the mouth . . . It's the angle and sharpness of the blow that does damage, anyway, not necessarily the force behind it.'

'Which is why a short left hook can put a boxer out for the count,' Andy agreed. 'Why two blows?'

'We'll think about it.' Bassett studied the dead man in silence. 'Poor chap,' he murmured.

The tiny office was barely large enough for three to sit in comfort, so Andy propped up the door jamb while Doc rinsed mugs under a running tap and Bassett, pipe filled but unlit, sniffed the milk.

'I'm late with the priest,' Doc said. 'Once cause of death was established for both of them I concentrated on the girl. Never did like the double suicide idea, but if she did want to die I wanted to know why. I was looking for alternative reasons.'

'Find anything?'

'No drugs or alcohol inside her. No bruising other than from manual strangulation; she was strangled "cold". No sex before death. In fact she wasn't promiscuous, far from it. Pregnant, yes; two months. No history of disease, hereditary or otherwise; no detectable organic disorder. Not HIV positive. An all-round perfectly healthy female.'

'An innocent taken advantage of,' Bassett murmured. He raised his voice: 'Possible, Jim?'

'Oh yes, it's possible. Time of death,' he went on. 'Can't be a hundred per cent accurate; can tell you this, though—she was almost certainly dead at seven-fifteen.'

Confirming what Bob Greenaway had intimated.

'Dead when driven away in Father Lambert's car. Died in her flat. Possibly in bed. *Not* a willing victim. She was taken unawares, asleep or dozing, hands underneath the sheets . . .' Bassett turned to Andy.

Who grimaced. 'Couldn't check the sheets for scratch marks, guvnor. Mrs Pugh-Talbot appeared while the photographer was in the flat. He asked her not to let anyone in but neglected to remind her to leave everything as it was. She had the bed stripped, linen sent to the laundry.'

'And anyway,' Bassett sighed, 'everybody thought the deaths were suicide. Never entered their heads to bag the bedclothes.'

Andy continued what had recently begun as an apology. Bassett waved the apology aside. 'Can't be helped. One of those things. At least we have photographs.' The prints he had examined earlier were sharp in his mind's eye.

'Those blows,' he said, lighting his pipe at last. 'Suppose Father Lambert went to Shirley on Friday evening as a priest. A priest only, on priestly duties. Disturbs the killer, who socks him on the jaw knocking him out. The killer then drives, dressed as the priest, to the picnic spot, the girl in the passenger seat, the priest curled up in the back.' He puffed smoke. 'Make sense?'

Andy waved his coffee mug in the air. 'How about the cut on top of his head?'

'How long to reach the picnic area—five minutes? He begins to recover consciousness, starts to sit up, our killer grabs—say the torch—strikes him again.'

Jim McPherson nodded. 'That would fit.'

'The boyfriend?' Andy suggested.

Bassett said, 'How did you get Shirley's medical history, Jim? Was she your patient?'

'My old partner's.' He anticipated the next question. 'She was asked routinely if the baby's father would support her. Reply evasive. She didn't name him.'

'How was she? Mention abortion?'

'No hint whatsoever that she didn't want the infant. The

reverse: she seemed confident the future would sort itself out. How wrong she was, the wee lass . . . When you've finished your coffee come and look at her hands.'

Nice hands. Capable hands. Smooth and well cared for . . . except for the tips of some of the fingers, and the fleshy part near the nail of the left forefinger.

Bassett was intrigued. 'Hand sewing without a thimble or finger guard. I've seen Mary's hands like that.'

'Sewing where?' Jim McPherson said. 'She earned her living doing casual work, they say. And Mrs Pugh-Talbot does own fashion shops—'

Andy took that up. 'Sewing for one of her suppliers?' He looked at Bassett. 'Could be how she met the boyfriend. Tailor. Rep. Agent. How do these things work?'

Or could be what Mary would have called 'trousseau stitching', Bassett thought. Did girls sew for their bottom drawers nowadays? Some, surely.

After the hands, the face. Even in death the girl was beautiful.

Outside, a few minutes later: 'I drew a picture back there, Andy, of Father Lambert arriving unexpectedly at the flat. Wrong, methinks.' He explained about the telephone call the priest had made before leaving the presbytery. 'Who else would he have spoken to but Mrs Pugh-Talbot, since she was—supposedly—alone in Briony House?'

'You think she wasn't alone?'

'I think—' Bassett broke off; began again. 'The boyfriend Shirley could never marry. What if he was already married, promised to divorce his wife, backed down when it came to the crunch? What if Shirley tried a form of blackmail? Hmm? Why do you strangle someone? You strangle someone you hate—if only at that particular moment. It wouldn't have taken a lot to kill Shirley, a slip of a girl. And if she was asleep . . . little resistance . . .'

The length of Glevebourne's short high street lay before

them. 'Don't go in much for fashion shops these days.' No Mary to buy for. 'Underpants and new socks are about my limit. Where 'tis, this boutique? Point me in the right direction, I'll walk, Andy.'

CHAPTER 7

The Glevebourne shop was the smallest of Mrs Pugh-Talbot's boutiques, but here, close to home, was where she had her office.

Sirens on glossy fashion magazine posters, there to lure, and their paper charm not altogether lost on him, escorted Bassett up luxuriously carpeted stairs to a plush spacious reception area, and the secretary. She was young, slender, her black hair was pinned and rolled ballerina-style, and she wore what Bassett gathered from the posters was fashionable black and white. She apologized politely: Mrs Pugh-Talbot couldn't possibly see him today.

Best smile, and, 'Would you let her know I'm here. I don't mind waiting.'

'It isn't a matter of waiting. She's due at Evesham, and she's late.' Nevertheless the secretary was beginning to unbend. He had such a cuddly face, was so gentlemanly. (This was Bassett's 'getting tough'. This and persistence. Which usually paid off. As it did today.) 'What did you say your name was?'

'Bassett.' He wrote it down: the whole mouthful.

'Oh.' Unconcealed interest now. 'Police. I'll see what I can do . . . Mrs Pugh-Talbot will see you presently,' she said, returning. 'Take a seat,' she invited.

He watched her get through to Evesham, tell 'Suzanne' Mrs Pugh-T would be late; contrived to catch her eye, and drew her attention to a poster, one of half a dozen decorating the walls like paintings in an art gallery. 'I like that! Mmm. The simpler the garment the bigger the price, my wife was accustomed to say. Does that still hold true?'

'That is the most expensive in the room.' Eyeing the poster sidelong.

'I might have guessed!' Bassett congratulated himself. 'Do you have your own designers and workshops?'

'No, we buy in.'

'Exclusives.' Having searched his memory for the word.

'Exclusive to this region. Your wife would have to be very unlucky to meet someone wearing the same design.'

'What about alterations?'

'We have a tailor and dressmaker we can call on, but we rarely use them. A garment is either right or it isn't, if you know what I mean. Why do you ask? Does your wife want something altering?'

'No, no. I'm a widower.'

'I'm sorry.'

So am I, my dear; so am I. 'No, no. I was thinking of a young lady friend who is handy with a needle.'

'And can't get a job?' The secretary screwed up her mouth in sympathy. 'Awful, isn't it?'

Her professional voice had slipped into everyday tone. A few minutes longer and Bassett could have been chatting and gently probing. Alas, a buzzer sounded.

'For you.' Professional voice back. 'The green door round the corner there—'

As Bassett disappeared she thought: Strange. She had felt certain he had come about Shirley. Although he *had* written down *ex*-Detective . . .

All the same she might eavesdrop.

'Your card says ex-Detective Chief Superintendent. Are you in Crime Prevention? Shop Security?'

She might have been one of her own models, Bassett

opined. Blonde hair exquisitely groomed, crimson suit beautifully tailored; crisp white blouse; a neat ankle—glimpsed as she returned briskly to her desk, for she had been at the door to greet him. Gold on both wrists, her ears, and at her neck. Tasteful gold. She was every inch a successful businesswoman.

'I'm retired, Mrs Pugh-Talbot, and making inquiries privately into the death of Father Lambert.'

'Oh.' Her mouth shaped a smile. Somehow it spoilt her; it seemed artificial. 'I understood when I spoke to the police that their questions were mere formality.'

'And you are not obliged to answer mine. I should be grateful for your cooperation, however. When doubt has been cast . . .' Bassett tapered off with a tiny shrug.

Began again. 'I'm trying to establish *when* Father Lambert arrived at Shirley's flat. There seems to be some difficulty about that. You saw Shirley at five-thirty p.m. May I ask what you did then?'

'I can't see what bearing it could possibly have on anything; he must have arrived to have left. But very well. I made a drink, relaxed with a magazine to unwind. My husband wasn't due home until eight so I was in no hurry. I went upstairs to run a bath, decided to look in to see if Shirley was feeling better, and to tell her there was cold chicken in the fridge. You know what young girls are like, if it's a toss-up between buying clothes or the latest in make-up or perfume, food loses. There is nearly always food going spare, I try to see that Shirley gets it.'

'But you couldn't get to her, the access door to the flat was bolted.'

'You know about that?' Mild surprise. 'I knocked, yes. Called. I think she heard me, all went quiet.'

'Yet she didn't come to the door. Did you go and try her front door? She had been poorly an hour before.'

'Gracious, no. She was obviously up and about. I called

to her about the chicken and left it up to her. I had my bath, dressed, went for a wander round the house. I'm a working woman, I don't see near enough of my home. The place had been made ready for weekend guests, it was a pleasure to go from room to room. I got to the drawing-room, put a light to the fire, and was looking out of a window when I saw Father Lambert and Shirley leaving.'

'No third person in the car?'

'Not that I could see.'

'You hadn't been expecting Father Lambert yourself? I ask because he is believed to have telephoned the house, not the flat, shortly before six o'clock.'

'I had no such call. And there was no one else in the house.' She frowned. 'Six o'clock. Where would I have been? I *did* go to the cloakroom. I wouldn't have heard the phone in there.' She smiled. 'There's the answer. He got no reply so decided to come in person.'

'Queer thing to do,' Bassett said reflectively. 'To phone you, then promptly drive here to do what they say he did.'

'Not me,' Mrs Pugh-Talbot said after a short silence. 'Shirley. He probably assumed, at that hour, that Shirley was in the kitchen fixing herself a meal.' And when Bassett twitched an eyebrow: 'She wasn't simply a tenant, she had become almost one of the family.'

'Which is why you let her stay on in the flat.'

'Why, yes. She had been extremely good to my mother. I owed her far more than the tenancy of a flat. Also, she was helpful in other respects. My husband and I go away a great deal. We have burglar alarms but it was an advantage having Shirley there during the day, to look after shutters and generally let herself be seen, so that the house never *looked* empty.

'Not that it always worked,' she went on with a touch of humour. 'We were burgled in July. Uncle Bertie's fault, though, he left a door open.'

'Much stolen?'

'Three items. An opportunist thief, apparently.'

Bassett voiced his regrets. Then: 'If I might recap about last Friday. You saw the car leave at seven-fifteen.'

'About then. It was getting dark but the drawing-room overlooks the top of the drive which is well lit.'

'Who was nearer to you?'

'Shirley, in the passenger seat. She had a scarf I bought for her draped round her shoulders. I recognized the colours. Father Lambert was driving.'

'You saw him clearly.'

'I could tell it was him. He was wearing his black. Certainly his hat. He was fond of his hat. And he was not himself; his driving was quite erratic.'

'Were you surprised when you saw them together?'

'Yes, I was.' Mrs Pugh-Talbot looked down at the gold pen she was toying with on the desk top, and up again. 'No, not surprised, taken aback. Shirley had told me the day before about the baby. I'd had no choice but to give her notice to vacate the flat. I exerted no pressure, she had a month or two's grace, but when I saw her with Father Lambert—I—I remembered the sounds I'd heard—I thought she had been packing her bags.'

'Was that when you went to the flat?'

Mrs Pugh-Talbot gave a small hollow laugh. 'You seem determined to get me into the flat. Yes,' she said with a sigh, 'that was when I went to the flat. It seemed rather discourteous of Father Lambert to have come to the house and pay me no heed. As if I was of no consequence in my own home. I didn't want to believe he would be a party to anything underhand, but if Shirley had been sensitive—over-sensitive—and had spun him a yarn—'

'I understand,' Bassett said. 'One thing puzzles me, however. You gave Shirley her marching orders on Thursday, yet on Friday you asked her to help with a charity show you were putting on.'

'I was trying to make amends, Mr Bassett. I wanted to let her know I was no longer cross with her. Which is why I was a little upset when I saw her leaving.'

'I get you. You were afraid she had walked out before you had time to make amends. Did she agree to help with the show?'

'I didn't get round to asking her. She had a headache if you remember. She would probably have turned me down. But at least I would have made the gesture.'

'True. Did you touch anything in the flat?'

'Literally? A wardrobe door. Drawers. I soon saw that she hadn't gone for good. Her suitcases were there, her toilet bits and pieces. Her toothbrush.'

'Did you notice anything different from when you were there at five-thirty?'

'The knife. It was missing.'

'Observant of you,' Bassett praised.

'Not really,' she said. 'The knife had been lying on a folded orange-coloured cloth; the same splash of colour drew my eye the second time. The knife wasn't there.'

'Did you think to wonder where it was?'

'I assumed it had been put in a knife drawer.'

'Do you recall the bed, Mrs Pugh-Talbot?'

'The bed? It was unmade.'

'But not untidy—'

'Shirley had got into it fully dressed. She hadn't gone to bed, she was only nursing a headache.'

Fully dressed. Bassett made a mental note.

'The bedclothes had been flung back from one corner,' he continued. 'You didn't touch it? No? If you had you would have seen a handbag, contents strewn.' He pulled on his bottom lip. 'Another puzzle. The bag had apparently been tipped out while Shirley was in bed. When she flung the bedclothes back—' He demonstrated. 'Bag and contents were covered over. Sandwiched. What might she have been looking for—?'

'Aspirin?'

'No aspirin bottle, no water glass by the bed.' No aspirin inside her, according to Jim McPherson.

'A comb.' Impatience was beginning to show.

'Comb on the dressing-table. Pen and paper? Both in a bedside drawer. Was she transferring items from one bag to another? No bag with her when she was found. Keys? Nought but a handkerchief in her coat pocket . . . What on earth was so important that she had to find it while she was in bed?'

'What do you think she was looking for, Mr Bassett?'

'A diary, photograph, piece of jewellery. I also have a suspicion that it was somebody else who did all the searching. You remember I mentioned a third person?'

'In the car.' A tiny frown came and went.

'Shirley had a boyfriend, a secret lover. And I for one do not subscribe to the view that her unborn child was Father Lambert's.' He hesitated. 'Do you?'

Her gaze was penetrating. Told him nothing.

'So.' He smiled, a trifle sadly, a shade resigned. 'Thank you for giving me your time. I'd like a word with your household staff, if I may,' he said, standing up.

She didn't demur. 'Of course.' She rose to show him out. 'Although Helen is the only one Shirley is likely to have confided in about a boyfriend, and she insists the girl never named him. I questioned Helen myself at the weekend.'

'Helen. She is the maid—' Bassett halted to peer at a framed photograph on the wall near the door. 'This is you? You ride!' He glanced down at her hands.

'I used to ride. Haven't done so for many years.'

But the strength would still be there, in the wrists.

'Lovely horse,' he said. Lovely woman astride the horse. Rounder then than now; full of life and laughter.

'Great pals, Whisky and I,' she said wistfully.

She went with Bassett to Reception. 'Debbie, phone the house, please. Mrs Blest and Helen should be there. Tell them to expect a Mr Bassett.'

Thus Bassett was prevented from continuing his chat with the secretary. Thanks and farewells taken care of, his hat safely collected from the stand, he stepped silently and thoughtfully down the stairs to the street.

I questioned Helen myself at the weekend. Questioned Helen about the boyfriend. Why—when at the time the boyfriend was thought to have been the priest?

And, *There was no one else in the house.* Why had the lady deemed it necessary to repeat that?

Bassett pondered on.

Eva Pugh-Talbot watched from her window until Bassett came into view below. Then, all business, she flicked a switch. 'Debbie, get me Julian, if you will. He'll be at Westonby Park. Then you had better go to lunch.'

To her son Julian she spoke coolly. 'I want the truth. Did you ever give Shirley Hughes a present?'

CHAPTER 8

'They're all round the back!' The postman slowed his van as he drew level with Bassett, and stuck his head out. 'I don't think they'll hear the bell.'

The bell? Bassett threw a look towards the pillared front door. 'Thank you.' He didn't know this postie; if he had the man might have tipped him the wink that: They've got the kettle on! As it was, he popped a half-eaten biscuit in his mouth and drove on along the drive, leaving Bassett to poke fun at himself. He hadn't wanted to announce his arrival yet; he had been tracing on foot the route from the flat at the side of the house to a spot at the front of the house where Father Lambert's car might have been when Mrs Pugh-Talbot saw it on Friday evening.

'Another burglary, and I'll be seeing an Identikit of meself on Police Five. "Man seen wandering suspiciously in the grounds of Briony House . . ."'

The post van a red blob vanishing between the trees, Bassett shunted his Citroën roughly into position. A man in outdoor working clothes watched him from the closed-in, hedged side of the house.

Half an hour later Bassett had had a chat with the man, who turned out to be the gardener, and with Mrs Blest, the cook; and was standing in the drawing-room gazing out of a window at his Citroën. Even in daylight it would be difficult to see properly who was in the driver's seat; in near darkness, lamplight shining on to the passenger side, Mrs Pugh-Talbot would have been able to identify the girl's scarf, but identify Father Lambert? Debatable.

He was waiting for Helen Fletcher, the maid. In the meantime he reflected:

The gardener, Tommy Johnson, a man pushing forty, had little idea of what went on in the house, he maintained; he delivered garden produce and cut flowers as required, would now and then have a cup of tea with Mrs Blest, but his job was outdoors, he worked alone and he kept himself to himself.

Friday last? Yes, he was with Mrs Pugh-Talbot in the garden when Shirley got home from the Graylings'. He had knocked off himself soon afterwards. Mrs Pugh-T had strolled with him to the cut-flower beds to select blooms for her dinner-party. His shed was there, he'd collected his jacket; she had been with him when he locked up.

Had Shirley talked to him much? Shirley was friendly

with everybody, had been the reply. What had she talked about? Did she ever talk about her boyfriend? Boyfriend? the gardener had said sardonically. Why should she talk to me about *him*?

He had meant the priest. He knew of no other man in Shirley's life . . . And now, if Bassett didn't mind, he had a pond to clean out.

Bassett had thought he detected bitterness. Mrs Blest offered an explanation.

'Mr Johnson was dreadfully upset. He liked Shirley, and she liked him, thought him a nice, kind man. Which he is. He never says a lot, men don't, but I saw him having a little cry to himself. I think he was sweet on her on the quiet. Not that it would have got him far even if he hadn't been twice her age.'

Why was that, Mrs Blest?

'Well, she had her head screwed on. She was going to do her nursing training and work her way up from there . . . Mind you, she was like most of us at her age, restless; one minute she was all for a career—the next she would have been happy to settle for a husband, a family, and a home of her own. What she wanted most of all was to remove the stigma of being what she called a foster kid. She imagined the stigma, mind. We wouldn't have known who she was if she hadn't told us . . . Anyway, what did she go and do? Silly girl. The unthinkable!'

Came as a shock?

'What do *you* think? Yet, when I thought about it, she had used to go on about him. It was Father Lambert this, and Father Lambert that. She thought a lot of him . . . Still, a shock. Not that I'm religious myself, but there's the right way and the wrong way of going about things. They could have worked things out better, I say.'

About last Friday, Mrs Blest.

Yes, she had seen Shirley at five o'clock. 'That was the

last time I saw her. I've already told the police; how often am I going to have to repeat myself?'

Alas, they omitted to ask what Shirley said to you.

'Said goodbye. Passed the time of day, asked if I'd been making blackberry jam, she could smell it on me. Nice, she said . . .'

Mrs Blest had begun to look anxious. Eventually she told Bassett why. 'It's a mystery to me, it really is. The last I heard Shirley was booked with the Graylings on Saturday, a day out with the children. The very last thing I said to her was have a nice day tomorrow, and she answered we'll do our best. Then lo and behold—'

Yes?

'Come Saturday morning I thought I must have dreamt it. Everything had changed. She never had been going to the Graylings, Helen said. And Mrs Pugh-Talbot said she had given herself the weekend off.'

A tap on the door halted Bassett's meditations.

Helen Fletcher was older than Bassett had expected, about thirty-two or thirty-three. Dark-haired, buxom, bare-legged and country healthy. Wearing a white T-shirt, sandals, and a summer print skirt which picked up the colour of her hair, and of her eyes which were green.

Country healthy but timid. 'Sorry to keep you.'

'That's all right.' Bassett gave her a bright smile. 'Where shall we sit?'

'Could we go outside?' A french window opened on to a conservatory, then the private hedged garden. She nodded in that direction. 'I'd feel more comfortable.'

'So would I,' Bassett said effusively. 'My name is Bassett, by the way.'

'Mine is Helen. Mrs Blest says you have some queries to do with Shirley. I thought it was done with.'

'Not quite. There has to be an inquest.'

He followed her lead towards a winding path, shrubs, flowers. 'You were one of the first on the scene, I understand. Care to tell me about it?'

'As I told the other police, Mrs Pugh-Talbot asked me to work all day with a break in the afternoon, two till six. This was on Saturday, Mrs Pugh-Talbot had important guests. I was on the way to the post office at two o'clock, on my bike, when this woman stopped me, wanting a telephone, an emergency. I directed her to a public box farther on. She was in a car or I would have gone for her.

'I had to pass where—where it happened. I saw a woman in the field pacing up and down, as if she was in a state. I cut across to her, and—' She squeezed her eyes shut. 'I wish I'd never seen them. If only I'd, well, gone straight home I wouldn't have.'

'There was a young reporter. You spoke to him, told him who they were.' A calculated guess.

'Yes. I thought he was a weekender. A tourist or walker. By the time I found out he wasn't I'd blabbed out that I knew the girl, and her name.'

'What else did you tell him?'

'Nothing. I knew Mrs Pugh-Talbot wouldn't want her name brought into it so I shut up.'

'What about Suicide Pact?' Bassett said quietly.

Some seconds passed before Helen replied. 'That was me,' she said sheepishly. 'It just came out—I suppose it was because I knew about the baby and everything.'

'Everything? You knew about Father Lambert?'

'*No*,' she said, her voice strained. 'I wish I had kept my mouth shut from the beginning, but when I was there all I could think of was—there they both were, together. I think I thought Shirley had lied to me.'

'Lied about the baby's father? She had told you it was somebody else's?'

'*No*. She didn't tell me a name. I just never thought it would be Father Lambert.'

'Until you saw them together.'

'Together, dead. Yes.'

'You stayed until the police came.'

'I realized I must. I'd identified Shirley, they'd want to know where she lived. Mr and Mrs Pugh-Talbot might not like it, but they couldn't be kept out of it, could they? Better for me to give the police Shirley's address than have them poking and prying.'

'Quite a crowd had gathered,' Bassett said.

'Most of them had gone home.'

'You knew many of them, though.'

'Hardly anybody. Mostly they were from town. It's a popular picnic site.'

'An ideal Saturday afternoon outing for children and dogs and a football!' Bassett enthused. 'Make the most of the weather before winter sets in. A favourite of—what's her name? Mrs Blest's niece?'

'Jenny? Yes, she has been once or twice. She wasn't there on Saturday, though. She was in the car with Dolly's husband when he picked her up at two o'clock.'

Bassett nodded. Forget the niece.

They came to a low wrought-iron gate, a bench seat next to it. 'Shall we take five?' Helen said. They sat amid fragrance and birdsong. It was a pity not just to enjoy the surroundings, but needs must.

'Shirley's boyfriend—' Bassett began.

'She never told me who he was.' Helen turned round to look at Bassett directly. 'Honestly.'

'She told you *every*thing,' he cajoled.

'Not that. He was only ever The Boyfriend.'

Bassett pursed his lips. 'I'll be frank, Helen. Some people find it impossible to believe that Father Lambert and Shirley were lovers, despite what appears to be evidence to the contrary. I start to look into that evidence, and what do I find? Already I've discovered a discrepancy. One person tells me Shirley was booked with the Graylings on Saturday, another tells me she had the weekend off.'

'She was self-employed, sort of. She could do what she liked. She didn't have to ask permission.'

'A reputation for unreliability wouldn't get her far, would it? Granted, she might have changed her mind about working on Saturday, but I still have to be sure. If one discrepancy rears its head, so may others. Which will mean I'll have to start investigating all over again.'

'Oh, it wasn't like that!' Helen gave a nervous laugh. 'Mrs Pugh-T had a dinner-party arranged, very important to her. She wanted everything to be perfect, and she thought if she began chasing Shirley, trying to locate her, there might be an atmosphere.'

'Locate her? Tell me what happened. Better still—talk me through Saturday. Save me asking questions.'

Helen frowned, and began slowly. 'I started at eight. Mrs Pugh-Talbot was in her dressing-gown, in the breakfast room, telling someone on the phone that Shirley wasn't well. The door was open, she beckoned me in and put the phone down. Mrs Grayling had been on, she said, Shirley hadn't turned up. She'd thought of sending me, but Mrs G. said she'd cope.

'Then she asked me to make her a fresh pot of coffee, the one on the table was cold. When I took the coffee in she asked if I knew where Shirley was. I said no, but her car was there. I come via the back drive, straight to the kitchen, you see. Me being dense, I didn't twig. I'd heard her say Shirley was unwell; should I go and see if she was all right? I said. Rather me than Mrs Pugh-T, I thought, I was thinking of morning sickness, but I didn't tell Mrs P-T what I was thinking.

'Well, then she said: Shirley isn't in her flat, Helen, she's taken French leave. But she didn't want the weekend ruined, so if anyone should ask I was to say it was her—Shirley's—weekend off.'

'Mrs Pugh-Talbot didn't say anything about Shirley having warned her the night before?'

Helen shook her head. 'No. I got the impression she was annoyed, felt let down. It was through Mrs P-T and a doctor that Shirley got most of her jobs.'

'She didn't say anything about the baby?'

'No!' Horrors! 'She didn't know! Shirley wasn't going to tell her until the time was right.'

'Meaning what?'

'When she had somewhere else to go, I suppose.'

'And the coffee-pot was cold, you say.'

'What was left in it. Mrs P-T had drunk most of it.'

Half a pot of coffee, cold by eight a.m.

'Can we get out this way?' Bassett said, tossing a glance towards the wrought-iron gate. 'I'd like to see Shirley's flat now, if I may.'

CHAPTER 9

The wrought-iron gate opened on to the edge of a shrubbery at the top of the drive. Rounding the shrubbery, Bassett stood taking stock . . . Drive on his left, its beginnings marked by gateposts that no longer supported gates; the long front of the house and a vast expanse of gravel away to his right; his Citroën from this distance dwarfed.

In his statement Uncle Bertie had said Father Lambert's car had narrowly avoided hitting a gatepost. Also that he, Bertie, had entered the house by the side gate.

Bassett turned to Helen. 'Is this the gate Bertie uses when he's been out with the dogs?'

It was. 'He refuses to use the old tradesmen's drive on principle,' she said gaily.

Eyes probing gaps in hedges as they progressed towards the house gave Bassett other entries and exits: to the conservatory, the garden room, rooms whose use he could but guess at. There were concealing hedges, foliage, and—ah!—as they reached the wide steps to the front door—a second low wrought-iron gate set in a box hedge growing right up to the front of the house. People could have come and gone all night without seeing one another.

He was thinking of Mrs Pugh-Talbot and Uncle Bertie, one arriving, one leaving at roughly the same time. In his mind's eye Mrs P-T should have left by the front door, it being nearest the drawing-room, should have spotted Uncle Bertie, waved, called to him.

According to their statements this hadn't happened. Nor had either mentioned seeing the car until the following day, when they were questioned by the police. Still, a matter of seconds would have made a difference; and if Mrs P-T wanted to avoid Uncle Bertie anyway . . .

Bassett froze momentarily. Why had he suddenly had that thought? He let it go. It was but a thought.

He turned his attention to the panoramic view the front of the house presented. He had been to the scene of the crime, could pinpoint the beauty spot from here; nevertheless, he asked Helen: 'How far away was Father Lambert's car found?' because he also wanted to inquire where she lived, and Uncle Bertie, and the gardener, and he wanted his curiosity to appear casual.

'There.' She directed his gaze to a line of poplars on a near-distant rise. 'About two miles. It dips down to woodland and a flat picnic area. I live over there.'

Bassett surveyed the overall scene. The two lanes ran parallel, fields in between, one the road to the post office, the other to Helen's bungalow. *If only I had gone straight home . . .*

If she had gone straight home she wouldn't have met the cub reporter and precious time would not have been lost investigating suicide.

'Twas but another thought.

He inclined his head to catch what she was saying. 'You can't see my bungalow from here . . .'

My bungalow. Her hands were ringless.

The gardener's home? She pointed. 'You can just see his roof and chimneys. In the same lane as me. My next door neighbour, you might say.'

There was a telling softness in her voice. 'Is Mr Johnson married?' Bassett inquired.

'No.' Helen blushed. An *understanding*, perhaps, he told himself.

They followed the house round to a midnight-blue door; hanging baskets on either side; brass doorknob and knocker: Shirley's flat.

Opposite the flat, a double carport built on gravel and Shirley's pink Mini. The gravel continued to a service yard and former coach houses converted to double garages; a separate single garage and the old tackle room flanked the approach to the former tradesmen's drive, which curved to join Helen's lane.

'I've got the key to the flat.' She produced it from a deep side pocket in her skirt. Bassett thanked her. 'Was the door locked on Saturday?'

'I don't think so. I think Shirley left the key on a table. From something Mrs Pugh-Talbot said.'

'And you didn't come to the flat on Saturday?'

'I would have if Shirley had been ill, but Mrs Pugh-T said she wasn't here, so what was the point? Would you like me to come in with you?'

'No,' Bassett said lightly. 'Tell me some more about the

boyfriend. What Shirley said about him. Or what you deduced for yourself. You must have been curious. I know I would have been if I'd been you.'

'She didn't mention him often.' All the same, Helen dug into her memory. 'He wasn't stingy—'

'Generous. Therefore possibly well off. Did he write to her, would you know?'

'Don't think so. The postie delivered her mail with the rest to the kitchen, and she was never on the lookout for a *special* letter.'

'Therefore they must have met. Where? Where did she spend her days off?'

'She never went far. Once or twice to London. Some times it was Hereford, Gloucester, Cheltenham. Mostly she went no further than Glevebourne.'

'*If word got out he would lose everything,*' Bassett quoted. 'So add status. We now know he may be well off, probably lives locally, and possibly has a certain position in the community—'

'*No.*' Helen rolled her eyes. 'That bit about losing everything—that applied to the baby's father.'

Bassett looked.

'It wasn't the boyfriend's baby,' Helen whispered.

'It wasn't the priest's either,' Bassett said.

A headshake, thin lips, and an expression of extreme self-loathing. 'You don't know the trouble I've had with my conscience after what I blurted out on Saturday. I knew it wasn't Father Lambert. I just didn't *think*.'

'Let me get this straight, Helen. You can't identify the boyfriend—but you do know who the baby's father is.'

'Shirley told me. She swore me to secrecy. I can't say; I promised.' She searched Bassett's face, seemed to make a decision. 'I can't *say*,' she said again. 'Besides . . .' She gestured. The house. 'I can't *say*—not with *Julian's* engagement to Penelope Westonby soon to be announced.' An eyelid fluttered: Had Bassett got it?

He had. Julian. The son of the house.

They began retracing steps to the flat door. 'The dinner-party on Saturday—'

'To meet the titled in-laws.'

'I see.' He looked rather weary, as if he wasn't sure whether to believe her or not, Helen thought. Should she go on, tell him more? For instance that Julian often called in via the back drive? At night, when his mother would be at the front of the house, and wouldn't hear him coming?

'There's something else, Mr Bassett—'

He listened, made no comment; put the key in the lock. 'Do you know what I'd love right now, if I'm not being too forward?' He affected his begging-bowl stance. 'A cup of tea.'

'Biscuits?' Amused, she started to fuss. 'Sandwich? I'll bring a tray. There's a door at the end of Shirley's corridor. Slide the bolt, save me having to come all the way round.'

The flat was upstairs. A single large room on the ground floor housed garden furniture, stacked chairs and trestle table, a folded marquee, and miscellanea.

The flat was neat, compact. Modern furnishings. Bathroom, kitchenette and airing cupboard on one side of the short corridor, sitting-room and bedroom on the other. The splash of orange on the kitchen table caught Bassett's eye, too; otherwise this room and the bathroom revealed only Shirley's tastes in food and perfumes. In the sitting-room: a conventional three-piece suite, tables, sideboard; TV, radio, books, magazines; plants dying from lack of water. No sewing or workbox.

The sideboard contained a bag of knitting wool and a partly knit pink jumper, a battered Ludo, ditto Scrabble, and clutter that accumulates simply from living. In one of the drawers: writing paper, pens, and a collection of pay slips secured by a bulldog clip. In a second: a child's purse, a much-washed—much-loved?—doll, and a plastic attaché case filled with doll's clothes.

Something gripped Bassett's heart and squeezed. Her most treasured possessions? Were these all that remained of the girl's childhood? A lump came into his throat.

He left the bedroom till last. A bedroom is a private place. Here would be the secrets, if secrets there were.

The unfairness of it all tore at him anew when he came upon a shabby canvas holdall heavy with school books; not from Shirley's childhood, these had belonged to now—her attempt at bettering herself. On the cover of an exercise book was a childlike: 'This work is the property of Shirley Anita Hughes.' It was dated three months ago.

He flicked through the books, shook them for letters or cards hidden or used as markers. Only one scrap of paper fell out: a receipt from Phoenix Fashions—'Coat, £40.00'. He put the receipt on the bed, the books back in the bag, and turned to the wardrobe, which was huge, semi-fitted, and boasted four doors.

Half empty was what he had expected. Not so.

So many clothes! How did a teenager, not long into a working life, come to own so many? Quality clothes, too. Most young people of Bassett's acquaintance bought cheap today, cheap by their standards, and discarded tomorrow, indicative of a throw-away society. Yet here were suits, coats, skirts, blouses . . . shoes . . . scarves, gloves . . .

Had Shirley benefited from discounts, compliments of Mrs Pugh-Talbot?

Even so—a nineteen-year-old. Who ran a car, an expensive item. What did the girl earn, for heaven's sake!

Or did she have the boyfriend to thank? A boyfriend who wasn't stingy. Clothes . . . car . . . What else? The bed had been stripped down to the mattress; Bassett pictured it made up, a handbag tipped out. Jewellery? *Traceable.*

Might have been if he had found any. His search came up with only costume jewellery.

He had emptied out the bottom of the wardrobe, lining up shoes and other things on the floor, and was rummaging through a bag of sewing scraps when he heard Helen at the access door. He dashed into the corridor to meet her; not quite quickly enough. Even as he was thanking her for the tea-tray and she was replying it was her pleasure, she was also craning to see through a crack in the bedroom door.

'Smashing lot of clothes she's got, hasn't she? You might have an outsized wardrobe! I used to say, but that's no reason to fill it!' Helen laughed at her own wit.

'Ah, they are all Shirley's own?' Bassett remarked. 'I thought some might belong to a friend who came to stay.'

'Oh no. She never had a friend to stay, anyway.'

'Roomy flat,' Bassett continued conversationally. 'Will they let it? Furnished, I imagine. What about the television and radio?'

'They were Shirley's. She bought them at Jones's. She's done nothing but spend since she got here!'

'Car, clothes, radio, television set,' Bassett said to himself, when Helen had gone. He put the tray on the bed, completed his search of the wardrobe, poured himself a cup of tea, and sat in the bedside chair to drink it, deep in thought.

A refill he left until he had rung up the station.

'Andy, I'm in Shirley's flat. Could you tell me what was taken from here apart from the handbag?'

'Letters and cards. We compiled a list of her foster parents and friends from them.'

'That all?'

'Hang on—' The sergeant made as if to put the phone

down. Bassett forestalled him. 'Get the info. Then how soon can you be here?'

'If it's urgent, fifteen minutes.'

He made it in twenty.

CHAPTER 10

'Letters dating back several years,' Andy informed Bassett. 'Plus two diaries, this year's and last. Diaries no help, the novelty had worn off by March in one, February in the other. Only other entries were birthdays. Looks as if she transferred them from one diary to the next.'

'Birthdays. Names?'

'Initials mainly.'

'Job for somebody. Match initials to names in the letters, see if we've any left over. Nothing else?'

'Nothing else worth taking, guvnor.'

'Exactly, Andy. She ran a car. Where are the papers: registration, MOT, insurance documents? There are pay slips here, presumably from when she worked full-time nursing Mrs Pugh-Talbot's mother; probably made up with the shop wages. Monthly, paid directly into a bank. So where is her bank book, cheque-book? Statements. Driving licence. Medical card? Where is her engagement book? She got work through Mrs Pugh-T and a doctor. Where are her records? Possible she trusted to memory, but I'd have thought there would be at least a notebook somewhere, by the telephone—'

Bassett stopped, motioned. 'The flat is neat, tidy. She had an orderly mind. She must have kept some kind of record.'

He drew Andy to the wardrobe. 'Black shoes—black handbag. Blue shoes—blue bag. Maroon shoes—maroon bag. But all the bags are small—for dress-up occasions. The remaining shoes are mostly brown and flat-heeled. What I would call everyday shoes. Where is her everyday handbag? The one that normally holds everything but the kitchen sink, as they say? It wasn't the one on the bed, too small.'

Andy nodded. 'Find the missing bag—'

'And we may find a few answers.' Bassett winked hopefully. 'We'll get a description before we leave.'

He pointed to the clothes. 'No bottom drawer stuff, unless this is it. Where did she get the money to buy this little lot, Andy?' He picked up a black plastic rubbish bag. 'This answers the sewing question. She had to shorten most of the clothes. The bits she cut off are in here. Beautifully done!' he praised. 'She knew how to sew.'

He handed Andy the receipt. 'Paid cash. But if she is a regular customer, be interesting to find out if she had an account and who settled the bills.'

'Phoenix Fashions. They're second-hand, guvnor,' Andy announced. 'My Joanna shops there occasionally.'

'Joanna?' Bassett put in. 'Same one?' His smile was warm. 'Serious?'

'I think so,' Andy said with masculine shyness.

'Good for you. Go on. You were saying?'

'As Joanna explains it, some women have more money than sense. They buy an outfit, wear it once, twice, or never if they can't slim down to it—and take it to Phoenix Fashions. Upmarket second-hand. The shop sells on commission basis. Joanna's had a fair few things at less than half they'd have cost brand new.' He tapped the receipt. 'You wouldn't buy a quality coat new for forty pounds.'

'You know, you're right. Bought a supply of underwear the other week. Cost as much as a three-piece suit and a spare pair of trousers cost a few years ago!'

'More than a few years, guvnor.' Andy grinned.

Bassett tut-tutted and laughed at himself. 'Behind the times is what I am. All the same, have a look. Add up to a bob or two even second-hand, wouldn't they?'

Andy agreed.

Bassett told him about his talk with Helen Fletcher. 'She says Julian Pugh-Talbot was the baby's father. Shirley told her so—and swore her to secrecy.'

'Julian? The son and heir?'

'Yes. Awkward for him if true: the Saturday dinner-party was in honour of his future in-laws.'

'You said "if true".' Andy flicked an eyebrow.

'Too pat for my taste, Andy. Want to make a note?' Bassett paused, then: 'One, identity of boyfriend remains a mystery. Two, boyfriend was *not* the baby's father. Three, nor was Father Lambert. Four, Who is? Julian Pugh-T? Head that: According to Helen Fletcher.

'Now, let's think. A secret boyfriend. How can you live among people for eighteen months or more and keep a boyfriend a secret. Not easy. Also, if you don't want to make him known, why mention him in the first place?'

'Maybe he doesn't exist, guvnor.'

'A figment of her imagination? I might agree if she hadn't kept up the pretence for so long. To prolong the tale of a boyfriend tucked away—I can't help feeling the tale must have some truth in it. I'm right in saying she appears to have had him since she came here?'

'So say her friends,' Andy said. 'Gives us the boyfriend finding out she's carrying some other bloke's baby. Pays her a visit, does her in.'

'Makes sense on the face of it,' Bassett said. 'The priest arrives, he has to die too. Why?'

'Recognized him.'

'Again, makes sense.'

'There aren't many people who'd kill a priest. Unless they were pretty desperate.'

Bassett nodded. 'Implies a murderer well known to the priest. Not just a face to describe to a police artist.'

'Someone close, in other words.'

Another nod, and a rub of his putty nose. 'Helen, the gardener, Mrs Pugh-Talbot, even the cook—they're all holding something back. Helen, for instance, says she knew everything. Next second says she knows nothing. Except, without undue pressure from me, the identity of the baby's father. Julian Pugh-Talbot.'

He walked over to the bag of school books, then the wardrobe. 'Education. Clothes. Ambitions. On the way up, wants to make something of herself, to further the good name she has already earned for herself. Yet she tells Helen, who, it's obvious to me is not to be trusted. Moreover, who works for the Pugh-Talbots.'

'She did tell Mrs Pugh-Talbot she was pregnant.'

'Did she? I have my doubts.' Bassett groaned. 'I'm in a bad way, Andy. I don't believe any of them.'

If he sought sympathy he didn't get any.

'Seriously,' Bassett said, after they had made faces at each other. 'The school books. Was she studying here, or attending a polytech? We need to know. We also need to know where she was getting the money to buy this little lot. Plus TV etcetera. A list of the men in her life, no matter how tenuous the connection—'

Started a list, Andy told him. 'Obvious from the nature of her work that she went into a variety of homes and institutions. No records, but Mrs Pugh-T was able to help. She gave us details going back six months. They're currently being checked out.'

'Good. Best put these things away as I found them. And water those plants . . .'

They continued to talk as they worked.

No joy with the cub reporter's camera, Andy said. He took some snaps of the death scene but packed it in when people started to crowd round. 'I saw what he did get; no use to us anyway. OK for his own black museum, I dare say. Fuzzy as hell, bad case of camera shake. He'll have to do something about controlling his emotions if he wants to be a paparazzo!'

Nor could the youth tell them who was there; powers of observation had been dulled by the occasion.

'Carried away by a surfeit of zeal, and spurred on by malevolent whispering,' Bassett mused aloud. 'I think I know who started the whispers, Andy.' He recounted the admissions made by Helen Fletcher. 'Says it was done in all innocence. Trouble is, she's had several days to get her story straight.'

Finished, they surveyed their handiwork. Tidy.

Tidy?

Bassett moved thoughtfully to the top of the stairs. 'Long flight of steps, Andy. The priest wore black shoes, right? There should be traces of shoe polish. If he was dragged down the stairs, that is.'

More thought. 'The girl was a light-weight. Carrying her down would present no problem. The priest was a heavy-weight. Unconscious. Therefore all arms and legs. If he wasn't dragged down the killer must be exceptionally strong. Or else had help. And his helpmeet could have been a woman.'

He turned. 'Let's go ask about that everyday bag.'

Helen thought the police must have taken it.

Afterwards Bassett was to ask himself why she paled when she saw Sergeant Andy Miller. Was it because she wasn't expecting to see Bassett with a *proper* policeman?

CHAPTER 11

'What do you know about the Graylings?' Bassett asked, as he and Andy trod gravel to their cars.

'Mum's a lawyer, dad's got a top job with an overseas aid charity. Absent for long periods, if you're thinking of Shirley.'

'Whereabouts are they?'

'A mile past the beauty spot. Big modern house named The Warren.'

Modern, but with ancient hedge and remnants of an old stone wall topped with cascades of purple aubretia flanking a short drive up to the house. Marigolds, nasturtiums, roses and fuchsia lined a path. Old oaks and a splendid chestnut graced new lawns which swept round to the rear of the house. New trees in protective coverings elsewhere.

Sounds of activity and children's laughter drew them towards the oaks and the garden beyond. Children, dogs, and a tall, white-haired, bearded gent sporting white trousers and linen jacket, fanning himself with a Panama hat.

'Uncle Bertie,' Andy said, voice low. A young woman in pale blue: 'The nanny.' Another woman, plump, short dark hair, cream skirt and coffee-coloured top; no spectator, a participator in the fun, she and Nanny might have been—but weren't—sisters: 'Mrs Grayling.'

She spotted them. Smiling, she sent the child holding her hand to Uncle Bertie, who now had the ball. 'Nip and take her place, Andy; play Hunt-the-Boyfriend. Shirley was relief nanny, might have said more to a fellow nanny than to—' Bassett broke off, doffed his hat. 'Mrs Grayling?'

A minute later Paula Grayling was directing Bassett

away from the merriment towards the quiet of pillars and vines, and a patio that looked enticingly cool.

'It was a dreadful shock. So sudden. We'd no idea!' Paula Grayling's voice was tinged with lasting surprise. 'I was thinking only this morning how dulled our natural senses have become. My maternal grandmother could tell a woman was expecting before she knew it herself. We seem to have lost all that, don't we?'

'Shirley should have been spending last Saturday with your children, I understand.'

'Yes. Zoë, our nanny, was over the worst by the middle of the week, but children are very demanding, the girl needed some rest, so I sent her home for a few days. Shirley was a boon. So handy having her to fill the breach.'

'Except that Shirley cancelled on Saturday.'

'Eva did.'

'Sorry?' Bassett feigned ignorance.

'Eva Pugh-Talbot. Shirley should have come with us on Saturday. We planned to set off at seven a.m. About half an hour before, six-thirtyish, Eva rang up to say Shirley was under the weather, dashed inconvenient, should she get Helen to come instead? I thought the girl had caught Zoë's bug.' She treated Bassett to a frank smile. 'Anyhow I knew Eva had a busy day ahead so I said no, not to worry, we'd cope. I realized afterwards that Eva had been covering for Shirley, she'd thought she had gone AWOL.'

'Mrs Pugh-Talbot rang you up, you didn't phone her?'

'Oh no. Shirley wasn't expected until just prior to take-off. Had she been late Uncle Bertie would have gone to fetch her. He was here at daybreak filling baskets and packing them into the waggon.' (The family nine-seater.) She smiled fondly. A happy woman.

Who seemed less happy when Bassett inquired: 'What time did you say Eva rang you up?'

'About half past six.'

'You sound uncertain,' Bassett said kindly.

Paula Grayling ceased walking. 'I don't mean to. I simply wonder why the questions?'

'My apologies, I should have explained. We're trying to ascertain Shirley's state of mind during the last hours of her life.'

'Oh yes. Yes. She did look tired when she went from here on Friday. Children *are* tiring. I can't honestly say I noticed anything else. It's so sad. If only she had been able to talk to someone. She could have talked to Uncle Bertie—'

This last was said with a nod towards Bertie, hobbling up to them a trifle breathless.

'—He's a kind gentleman, for all that he pretends to be a rascal sometimes.'

She raised her voice as Bertie came closer: 'You look all in! You're too old for rough-and-tumbles!'

He arrived. Wheezed a mock scold: 'Ha!' Stretched his lanky frame to full height. 'Drop o' highland oil is required, old girl, that's all.' To Bassett: 'Beats your vitamins and hormone rubbish.' Again to Paula, gazing at him as if his very presence was a delight: 'And a breather, I confess. Had the wind pummelled out of me.'

A long straight hand came out. 'Uncle Bertie—'

'Bassett.' The old gent's grip was firm.

'I'll get some drinks.' Paula Grayling began to go.

'I'll attend to them. Your turn out there.' Uncle Bertie pointed with his stick.

'Do I have to?' she begged playfully. Still, after a fake woe-is-me look at Bassett, she went.

'Grand woman, that,' Bertie informed Bassett. The stick pointed again. 'Shall we park ourselves?'

They did so at a table on the patio under a fringed umbrella, Bertie disappearing into the house first, to re-appear with glasses, ice, and a hip flask which he later restored to a pocket.

'Do you live here?' Bassett asked. He knew Bertie didn't, but it was as good an opener as any.

'Wouldn't dare! Might wear out me welcome!'

No relation, Paula and her husband, Bertie said, but good as gold to him. And he loved children. 'Fell for this place soon as I saw it re-named The Warren. Sense of humour. Great fun. Three little Graylings so far, bound to be some more.' He shot Bassett an ear-to-ear grin. 'Talk too much. Reputation for it. Best come to the point.'

He jerked a thumb. 'Couldn't help overhearing some of what your man was saying to Nanny Steadman. Sergeant, isn't he? Met him once. Broad shoulders, good face. Yes. Occurs to me the authorities aren't satisfied. If they were you wouldn't still be investigating. Am I right?'

'You're right,' Bassett replied.

'The infant? Or a whole lot more?'

'Some more,' Bassett said cautiously.

'Hm. Never did sound pukka. What're you after?'

'The identity of Shirley's secret boyfriend.'

'Thought it was the priest, found out it wasn't. That it? Know what's going to happen now, old man? More tragedy unless you get cracking. I speak of speculation. Shirley, single gel, gets herself in the family way, tongues wag. You get my drift?'

There was no animosity in Bertie's tone. He paused, studied Bassett as if taking his measure; said, 'Best have it out in the open. Speed things up if I tell you. If I don't another kind soul might. A bit of scandal a year or so ago, Rupert and a local woman. Blew over, but some folk are blessed, or cursed, with long memories.'

Long noses, too. Common knowledge in some quarters that Rupert and Evie lived separate lives. 'Point is—' Bertie leaned forward, confided man to man—'he learnt his lesson—too close to home. Told him—if you *must*, old man, stay away from your own doorstep. Little woman in

Town's the thing. Took my advice. Evie knows. Suits her. Leaves her free to live her own life.'

'You mean she has a gentleman friend.'

'If she has she's keeping quiet about him. No, I mean her dress shops. Rupert has his woman in London, Evie lives for her business. Weekends they play the game: they are the Pugh-Talbots, devoted couple.'

'What about Julian, more Shirley's age?'

'Never. Fine young man. Perfect gentleman. Besides, he's got his own gel, getting married soon.'

'Never stopped some hot-blooded young men,' Bassett said lightly.

Not so lightly Bertie replied, 'Could have fallen for Shirley? Possible. Anything is possible. Pretty little thing. Tell you this, though, if Julian was responsible for her condition she'd be alive today.'

'How about you, Bertie?'

'I should thank you for the compliment, old man. In case you're serious, yes, I was a notorious womanizer in my day, as you've no doubt heard; but I never messed with a youngster. My lady friends were of a kind, they knew where they stood. And it was a long time ago.'

The blue eyes were wearying, the moustache and beard weren't half as proud. 'Fond of Shirley. Lovely gel.' The eyes narrowed feelingly. 'Hope you get the bastard.'

'We will. Mind if we go over Friday evening again?'

The story didn't alter in the re-telling. Bertie had been returning with the dogs when the priest's car had nearly run him down. The time was 7.15 p.m.

'Get a good look at Shirley, did you?'

'Too busy saving me neck and glaring at the driver, till I saw it was a priest.'

A priest. 'You didn't actually recognize him?'

'Saw the black, the hat. Light from a lamp fell on him as the car flashed past . . .' Bertie faltered; sipped his drink.

'Made the old ticker pound a bit!' he exclaimed heartily.

'After you took the dogs in, what did you do?'

'Ohhh. Went to the library, poured meself a snifter—I needed one! Read the paper waiting for Evie to come down. Must've dozed off. Yes—' He speeded up. 'Heard Rupert. Woke me up. Don't like to intrude when he's home, so I pulled meself together and took me leave.'

'The time was then—?'

'Just turned eight. Clock in the kitchen. Guessed Evie would be there, went to say cheerio. Julian was with her, just come in, smelt of cold—'

They got no further: the children, nanny and Paula Grayling were trooping up to them. A small voice said, 'Is Uncle Bertie's friend staying for tea?' Some merriment followed, Bertie joining in loudly from the sidelines, till Bassett said, 'Could I have a word with the nanny, do you think?'

'Nanny Steadman!' Bertie beckoned cheerfully. 'I'll leave you to it. Come on, children, hands to be washed—'

'Shan't keep you long, Miss Steadman.'

'Zoë, please. It's only Uncle Bertie who insists on Nanny Steadman,' she whispered. 'He's very proper, the love.'

She was hot and flushed from play; and talkative. 'I've told the sergeant all I know, which isn't much, I'm afraid. I'm sure I told Shirley about *my* boyfriend, he's the person I dash home to when I'm off duty, but I honestly can't recall Shirley ever mentioning hers. She wouldn't want to, would she?'

Not if the priest was the boyfriend; which was what her look of distaste seemed to imply.

'What about girlfriends, Zoë? Any ideas?'

'Ummm, yes. I don't know her name, but the girl at the shop called Phoenix Fashions—Shirley was friendly with her. And a girl named Lisa. I remember her name because I have a sister, Lisa. And Debbie, Mrs Pugh-Talbot's secretary. I think they all sort of got together now and then. I can't think of anyone else.'

'Phoenix Fashions, Lisa, Debbie. Thank you, big help. Are you better now?' Bassett asked solicitously. 'You've had the 'flu?'

She was better by Wednesday, Zoë said. 'But Mrs G. is sweet, she sent me home for the rest of the week.' Her face clouded. 'We'll miss Shirley.'

'Yes . . .' Bassett cocked an ear. 'I hear children getting anxious. I'd better let you go. Good luck.'

Andy was waiting for him at the bottom of the slope.

'Wanted to meet her, Andy. Asked about Shirley's girlfriends. Lisa rings a bell from your files. Another is a girl who works at Phoenix Fashions. How did you fare? She said she couldn't help you much.'

'Depends,' Andy said as they fell in step. 'No help with a boyfriend, so I asked about men in general. She came up with one we didn't know about—a teacher. Whose name is Tommy Johnson.'

'The gardener?'

Andy grinned. 'He's a teacher. Or was, until he had a nervous breakdown eighteen months ago. Shirley wasn't going to a polytech, Johnson was coaching her in his spare time.'

'*Was* he now?' Bassett tapped his memory. *I think he was sweet on her on the quiet.* The cook, Dolly Blest, had said that. 'Have you checked out Uncle Bertie's story with the old retainer yet?'

'Not yet. Want me to pump her?'

'Yes. I thought Tom Johnson and *Helen*—'

'What did you make of Uncle Bertie?'

'Liked him,' Bassett said. 'He defended Rupert Pugh-Talbot, and Julian.' He gave Andy the gist. 'Then I had him go over Friday evening. He was at the house for roughly an hour after taking the dogs in; was there when Mr Pugh-T and the son got home. Apparently he saw nothing of Mrs in the interim.' He placed emphasis: 'Says he nodded off while waiting for her to "come down."

Andy flicked him a glance. 'His way of covering up the fact that she was missing for that hour?'

'Worth thinking about, Andy. Something else. Bertie didn't actually see Shirley, only an impression of her.'

'Meaning what, guvnor?'

'Meaning I'm satisfied the car did nearly run him down, he hasn't been kidding us. Also, that what he *thought* he saw is suspect, his mind might have been playing tricks. He saw *a* priest. More accurately, perhaps someone dressed as a priest. I have a funny feeling he wouldn't be able to put his hand on his heart and swear it was our Father Lambert.'

He smiled. 'Proves the value of persistence. Let folks know we are still investigating and closed minds open to the light. Bertie knows there was something not quite right about the occupants of that car. Doesn't know what, not yet, that is. We'll wait and see what develops.'

They had long since reached their cars. Bassett looked at his watch. 'I must go and see my dog. Then I want to try and catch Mrs Pugh-Talbot.'

Andy said he'd return to the office, and the mountain of work piling up higher and higher. He gave vent to a terrible to hear exaggerated moan. Which had Bassett grinning broadly. 'Go on. You love every minute of it, Andy.'

Bassett was half way to his widowed lady friend's when he recollected Bertie's *Julian was with her, just come in, smelt of cold* . . . He'd slipped up. He should have asked Bertie who had just come in—Julian alone? Or Julian and his mother, the two of them together?

CHAPTER 12

'Damnfool questions!' Bassett ticked himself off. 'If Andy says Julian was at the pub until eight o'clock, then Julian was at the pub until eight o'clock. Andy's good.'

He and his labrador were sprawled side by side on a slope of the Malvern Hills not far from Bassett's cottage. Man and dog were resting after a boisterous romp, the dog too exhausted to give better than a token thump with her tail in response to Bassett's monologue.

'You're right,' he said. 'So long as it's only myself I ask damnfool questions . . . Been wondering if the car was deliberately aimed at Bertie. What do you think?'

The big brown eyes swivelled, the beautiful head and body still reclining, even though that did sound a little like a promise. When nothing happened the eyelids drooped and the dog feigned sleep again; lessons in patience had been learnt long ago.

But the imagined promise was in due course honoured. 'Come on, Babydog, ten more minutes!' The dog was on her feet first, a writhing bundle of instant energy. And the ten minutes stretched to half an hour.

Thus it was well after six when Bassett drove on to an almost deserted shoppers' car park in Glevebourne. He was too late. He reached Phoenix Fashions only to find the shop had shut at five-thirty. Shut also, a few doors along, was Eva Pugh-Talbot's boutique. The cleaner was there, however, grey hair trilling a tune from Top Twenty, long earrings swinging merrily back and forth as she swept the step.

On the off-chance Bassett stopped and inquired if Mrs Pugh-Talbot was back from Evesham—and struck lucky.

'She should be here any minute. She phoned earlier. I'm to tell Julian. Are you . . . ?'

'No,' Bassett said amiably. 'Julian is her son.'

'Oh. I haven't worked here long, you see.'

'Enjoying it?' Bassett's eyes twinkled back at hers. 'Keeps me out of mischief!' she said. He would come back later, Bassett said. 'No need to tell Mrs Pugh-Talbot, in case I change my mind. Pleased to have met you.' Touching his hat.

Delicious aromas had been tantalizing his nostrils ever since he stepped from his car. Now his mouth positively watered: he was ravenous. He followed his nose across a now quiet dusty street and down a cobbled alley to a fish and chip shop; took his hot vinegar-scented parcel to the bench seat opposite the courtyard entrance to the boutique; and there rediscovered the unbeatable flavour of fish and chips eaten straight out of the wrapping paper.

A red sports car had been driven into the courtyard during Bassett's brief absence. He watched Mrs Pugh-T arrive in a blue Rover. Contrived to be passing when she and a tall, blond-haired Greek god emerged from the shop some time later. He wasn't ready for Julian, was glad when the young man pecked his mother on the cheek and tore off along the street.

'Fortuitous, Mrs Pugh-Talbot!'

She laughed a small, not altogether humourless, laugh. 'Are you sure you aren't doing what that scruffy little TV detective—Columbo—does? Hounds people?'

'Hounds his chief suspect, surely.'

She shrugged lightly. 'How can I help you?'

'A query has arisen about last Saturday morning . . . You told the police that Mrs Grayling phoned you to say Shirley hadn't put in an appearance.'

'I did not!'

'No, you did not,' Bassett reprimanded gently. 'You told

them that Shirley wasn't working that weekend. Not true. Moreover Mrs Grayling didn't have to contact you—you phoned her to say Shirley was under the weather.'

'A harmless lie, Mr Bassett.'

'And I am aware of the reason for it. What I cannot work out is how you knew before six-thirty on Saturday morning that Shirley would be indisposed.'

'I told you.' She reconsidered. 'All right—guilt, Mr Bassett. I told you I hadn't been as sympathetic as I might have been about the baby, that I thought when I saw Shirley leaving she was running away. I was worried. Also, I didn't want Father Lambert to think ill of me. I hardly slept a wink on Friday night. I listened and listened for her, dropped off eventually, and woke up just before six. I went round to the flat. I had the spare key but everything was as I had found it the night before, door unlocked, bed the same, everything. I waited till six-thirty. When there was no sign of her I knew somehow that she wouldn't be coming. So I phoned Paula. There was just time for me to have fetched Helen to go in Shirley's place.'

'What if she had gone directly to the Graylings' from where she had spent the night?'

'The onus would have been on her to explain,' Eva Pugh-Talbot said tetchily. She repented. 'Perhaps I ought to do some explaining myself. That about Paula phoning me. You will have got that from Helen. It was foolish of me to pretend Paula had that minute phoned, but Helen tends to surmise, and exaggerate. She would have thought there was something very odd about my going to the flat at first light.'

'You could have said you were making sure Shirley was awake in good time.'

'I would never have done that, and Helen knows it. I'd have used the telephone, if anything.'

'You weren't afraid of Helen surmising anyway?'

'She wouldn't have done it *aloud*. Not once she'd had it

drummed into her that Shirley was taking the weekend off after all. Helen will babble on, embellishing as she sees fit—unless you ask her not to say anything. Then she'll keep your most precious secret.'

Bassett raised an invisible eyebrow.

'And you wanted Shirley's disappearance kept secret? Do I understand correctly?'

'For that weekend, yes,' Eva Pugh-Talbot said intensely. 'If I'd started chasing her—Oh, to hell with it!' she said angrily. 'I'd washed my hands of her, for the weekend at any rate. Under no circumstances was I going to allow her to spoil my arrangements. That's the bottom of it. I am only too sorry that what I believed at the time was a simple white lie has caused so many problems.'

'No, no, no,' Bassett said charitably. 'It would've remained simple if it hadn't been for the tragedy. I have one other item for clarification.' He appeared to consult his notebook. 'Ah yes. Friday evening. Bertie got home with the dogs, couldn't find you—'

'He wasn't a *guest*, Mr Bassett. One didn't have to *entertain* him. If you must know, I needed to think. I had a horrid feeling the little minx was going to put a damper on my dinner-party. Sorry, I shouldn't have said it quite like that . . . The fact remains, it was to be an *occasion*, I wanted it to be perfect, and I could well do without any turmoil. So, I wanted to think, and to compose myself; I knew Bertie would have sensed my agitation . . . So yes—I was slow to go in to him. When I did he was asleep. I elected not to disturb him.'

'Fine!' Notebook away. 'Clarification received. Thank you.'

'May I go now?' Her good humour had been restored.

Alas, Bassett was to take it away again.

'I'd appreciate a word with your son. My telephone number.' He gave her the slip of paper, prepared while he sat on the bench. Added, as if informatively, 'We are beginning to get a picture of the elusive boyfriend. We think he may be a local man, moderately wealthy—'

'May you find him soon.' Her hand shook as she opened her handbag to stow the slip of paper, although her voice was well under control. 'I must go now, I'm very tired.'

A thoughtful Bassett headed for the car park. He had been made very aware of Eva Pugh-Talbot's self-control. And the effort it had cost her.

Late that night he telephoned Andy Miller.

'I've got something too, guvnor. The pub where the son spent an hour on Friday night? I've sniffed out something peculiar. Can't do anything about it now, I'll get on to it first thing in the morning.'

CHAPTER 13

Andy Miller was on the telephone to Bassett early the following morning.

'Bob's been on, guvnor. One of the foster mothers was visited by Shirley when the girl was working at the school. Apparently the family asked if she had a young man yet, as people do. The smaller children joined in. Shirley told them she had, his initials were F.P., could they say what the F.P. might stand for. They guessed Fairy Prince. Hang on—I haven't finished. Shirley laughed and told them they might be right! With me?

'The foster mum doesn't think Shirley was jesting. She asked Shirley herself, without wanting to pry, didn't press the issue in other words. From Shirley's reply she is convinced there was someone in Shirley's life—someone she wanted to keep secret, she'd tell them all in good time. According to the foster mum, Shirley was quietly over the moon, couldn't believe her good fortune. Lets out Father Lambert. She says Shirley wouldn't have boasted as she did if he'd been a priest.'

'Bob's going to the school, I take it.'

'Yep. He also has a line on Shirley's real mother. There's a strong possibility that Shirley's money was left to her by her grandmother. Oh, and there's no F.P. in the diaries, by the way. Can tell you the rest when I see you.'

They arranged to meet at midday for a pub lunch.

The girl at Phoenix Fashions was short-legged, round-faced, and might have been judged plain but for the most luxuriant head of hair—red-gold in colour—Bassett had seen in ages. Her name was Angela, her father owned the business, she was manageress; and yes, Shirley had been a good customer. Not that she had bought anything recently, mind.

'She was rather more than a customer, wasn't she? There was you, Lisa, Debbie—?'

'Well, yes, Shirley did come out with us sometimes.'

'How did you meet? The first time, I mean?'

'In the shop. Shirley came almost every week in the beginning. We got quite chatty. Then one day Lisa was here and Lisa chats to everybody. Five minutes with a stranger and you'd think they'd been friends for life.'

Bassett chuckled. 'Good for Lisa.' At last Angela smiled. It was a nice smile. Never plain! Bassett decided. Tom-boyish. He'd seen the freckles on the bridge of her nose.

'I'll tell you what I'm trying to find out,' he said confidingly. 'The name of Shirley's boyfriend.'

Angela stared. 'Wasn't it Father Lambert?'

'No,' Bassett said quietly. 'It wasn't.'

'Shirley never told us his name,' Angela said. 'I'm sure she met him before she came to this area.'

'Go on,' Bassett encouraged.

'It wasn't Father Lambert?' She seemed confused, yet half pleased. 'She was probably telling the truth, then . . . She mentioned him the first ever time she came in. She'd fallen in love with a cream suit in the window, fitted her perfectly, and I knew for a fact it had never been worn. She bought it, chuffed to death she was. Not sure my boyfriend would approve, she said; but you can't tell that it's second-hand, can you? What a bargain! She was looking at other things by then.

'I said the boyfriend needn't know, she could always pretend they'd been at the back of her wardrobe, forgotten. We had a laugh over it and, cutting the story short, she told me he was working abroad on a contract job. I asked what kind of job. The kind you don't talk about, she said. She wasn't rude about it. I imagined he was in Iraq or wherever, one of those supermen who go in under cover.'

'How long ago was this?'

'Oh, eighteen months ago, maybe longer.'

'She came in regularly after that?'

'Every week. Not always to buy, sometimes just for a look. She bought a lot overall, though. She wanted to look her best for him. She used the word "classy" often. Does this look classy? she'd say. Another time she said it was the best thing she ever did, finding my shop, she could buy quality clothes and have change to spend on the right accessories.'

'Did she tell you where she got the money to pay for them all?'

'I did once remark that she must have a good job. She told me a relative she never knew she had left her some money in a will. She said it was thrilling having money to spend, and how awful it must be for people who'd grown up with money suddenly to find themselves broke.'

'Did she have anyone in particular in mind?'

'I don't know. I thought she was speaking generally,

about redundancies and businesses going broke, that kind of thing.'

'Go on,' Bassett said kindly. There was more, he could tell.

'One day she wasn't as bubbly as usual. The boyfriend would be coming home soon, and she didn't know what to do. She had realized she couldn't marry him. Lisa was here and Lisa being Lisa—she said no problem, just tell him! To which Shirley being Shirley replied it wasn't that simple. But she wouldn't tell us why.

'We didn't see her then for about two months, until she dropped in one day to say hello. We asked if she had given him the ring back—'

'Engagement ring? She was engaged to the fella?'

'Well, yes. She had a super ring. Sapphires, diamonds, platinum. Must have cost a small fortune.'

Bassett puzzled silently. No ring mark on Shirley's finger. 'Had she given it back?'

'She said she hadn't.'

'She wasn't wearing it?'

'She hardly ever wore it, it lived in her handbag.'

'Strange,' Bassett said, making a face.

'Yes. I did wonder if she was ashamed of him.'

'Why ashamed?'

The lovely hair wafted delicate perfume as Angela averted her face, the better to think. 'It's hard to put into words,' she said, turning to look at him for a moment. 'But Shirley changed. When we first met she was teenagerish. Sort of too serious about some things, yet giggly and silly about others. You know? But the clothes weren't teenagerish. It was as if they epitomized what she wanted to be.'

'Classy?' Bassett smiled.

'Classy, yes! Smart. She sort of altered herself to suit the clothes, if you understand me.'

'She grew up. Matured.'

'More than that, even. Grooming herself to be a *lady*, is what I once thought. I wondered if associating with the Pugh-Talbots and people on their level had—you know—given her fresh ideas about the man she wanted.'

'Her fiancé no longer good enough? In spite of the expensive ring.'

'You don't have to be rich to buy your girl a decent ring. It could even have been stolen.' Angela seemed to regret this the second she said it. 'What I mean is, her fiancé was her first boyfriend. She didn't really know him. I imagine,' she added awkwardly.

'And she had since met other men, possibly more to her liking. Like Julian Pugh-Talbot, for instance?'

'Julian? *Like* Julian, possibly.'

Bassett gazed straight into her eyes. 'Did she fall for Julian, or he for her?'

'Oh no! Definitely not.' She crushed that notion out of hand. 'The boyfriend definitely wasn't Julian.'

Lisa Barrington lived in a neat detached house in a neat new cul-de-sac. The young lady herself was not so neat: she came to the door wearing grubby jeans and sweatshirt, her hair all over the place.

'Mr Bassett? Come in. Angela phoned.'

She scurried ahead to the living-room, and hurriedly swept papers, magazines and a duster off a chair for him to sit down. 'Excuse the mess. Mum, Dad and brother Dan are holidaying in Majorca, due home tomorrow, and I'll not get this place cleaned in time.' She screwed up her mouth and aped the harassed housewife, wiping invisible sweat off her forehead. 'Pity me.'

Bassett smiled. 'I pity you.'

She sank on to an armchair, pulling her long legs under her; had second thoughts, looked about, and: 'Drink?'

Bassett declined with a raised flat palm.

'It's no trouble.' Easing herself up.

'No, no. I have a lunch date.'

She curled up again. 'Who exactly are you?' she said. Forthright young miss.

'Retired police detective.'

'Investigating on behalf of Father Fitzroy.'

'Yes.'

'Trying to clear the two's names. How can you do it?'

'We're fairly certain the baby wasn't the priest's.'

'Whose do you think it is?' A frown. 'Was . . .'

Bassett ignored the question, as Lisa had known he would. 'Angela has been telling me about Shirley's fiancé.'

'Secret fiancé.' Accent on the secret. 'I took a lot of what Shirley said with a huge pinch of salt. Angela believes everything people tell her.'

'Shirley had an engagement ring.'

'Never let us touch it or try it on. Or hold it up to the light to see if the stones were real. Never showed us a photograph. Or a letter. I asked her if I could have the stamps for Dan, he collects foreign stamps. Admittedly I was testing her—' Eyebrows up. 'Never saw one.' And down again. 'Not one.'

'You thought she had made him up?'

Lisa jerked her head; it might have been a nod. 'My mother worked with a woman who invented a lover. She went the limit, bought herself rings, wedding dress, a going-away outfit—even got the girls in the office to help her with invitation cards.'

'Did this woman's romancing go on for as long as Shirley's? Eighteen months, maybe longer?'

'No.' Lisa backed down a little. 'She came in four days before the wedding and said they'd had a blazing row.'

'Which Shirley could have done. Tell me,' Bassett said,

'were you there when she said she realized she could never marry her boyfriend? What were her exact words?'

'I was teasing, asking if they'd set a date for the wedding. Shirley said there wouldn't be a wedding, she had realized she could never marry him.'

'Those were her words?'

'*I can't ever marry him, I realize that now.*'

'Yet two months later she still had his ring.'

'*Six* months later. I saw it in her bag a fortnight ago. She couldn't give it back, she said, she didn't want to hurt him.'

'She said that a fortnight ago.'

'No, I didn't let on I'd seen the ring then. It was what she was saying a couple of months ago. She had been saying it all summer. Six months.'

'Didn't want to hurt him,' Bassett repeated. 'What do you think she meant?'

Lisa shrugged: No idea. 'Unless it had to do with the money she'd been spending.'

'I understood she inherited that.'

'Left in a will, she *said. Do* Barnardo's orphans have relatives who leave them money? Whereas if *he* had sent it to her, well—it's a bit rough to spend it, then give the chap the bum's rush.'

'Orphans can have aunts, uncles, cousins.'

Lisa looked. 'Yes, I suppose so. I never thought of that. You think of orphans having nobody, don't you? I suppose those poor little kids in Rumania and Russia have relatives somewhere if anyone would bother to look.'

One caring thought led to others. In silence to begin with, then: 'We never did *quite* believe Shirley would—you know—go with a priest. We were flabbergasted when we were told. Yet when we talked it over . . .' Lisa hesitated.

'Carry on.'

'Well, in spite of what I just said about an imaginary boyfriend, an affair with the Father did seem to fit. Take the secrecy—for obvious reasons. He wasn't abroad—he just wasn't free. If he'd applied to leave the priesthood, and they were dragging their feet over—what do you call it? Dispensation?—that would account for the waiting period. In the end she didn't want him, but daren't tell him because the quitting-the-church procedure had gone too far. She wouldn't have hurt him, she'd have *destroyed* the man . . . I think I prefer the other one—spending a chap's money and running out on him.'

'Or spending her own money,' Bassett said quietly, 'and coming to realize her fiancé wasn't her Mr Right.'

Lisa nodded, slowly and thoughtfully. So thoughtfully Bassett asked himself what he had said to bring it on: there was undoubtedly some new thinking going on in her head.

'Do the initials F.P. mean anything to you?'

'F.P.' Lisa shook her head.

'One last question. Is it possible—think carefully—for Shirley to have changed her mind about her fiancé for one reason only, that reason being another man?'

'That's always possible,' Lisa said sagely. 'Happens daily. Accounts for the high divorce rate. Better to find out *before* the wedding . . . I can't see what the problem was, honestly.' Her eyes opened wide. 'Nobody sues if you quit an engagement, not these days.'

'Are you saying there *was* someone else? You've come up with a name? Julian Pugh-Talbot?'

'No. She liked Julian; *liked* him, that's all. She liked the teacher chap, Tom Johnson. She liked my dad when she came here once. She'd have liked you.'

'She liked men?'

'She liked people. People,' Lisa said. She swung her legs off the chair. 'You've got it all wrong!' she said as she stood up. 'Julian wasn't the father of the baby. No way. I'll have to ask you to go now, if you don't mind.'

'Of course.' Bassett was already on his feet. 'I've enjoyed our chat.' He spoke the truth.

Outside, he sat in his car, pondering. Angela had wondered if Shirley was ashamed of her boyfriend; Angela believed he existed. Lisa had not; in her opinion he was a figment of imagination. Until the tragedy, that is, when the priest had seemed to fit the bill.

Seemed to fit the bill. Yet no *great* surprise when he suggested Father Lambert was innocent. In any event, they had been *flabbergasted* when they heard the original story. They hadn't wanted to believe it . . .

Hmm. According to Angela, the boyfriend dated from before Shirley moved to Glevebourne. *Could* have been the priest. In Shirley's mind? An imaginary love-affair with a real priest? *Could* have been Julian; met him at the school, Oakdean. Well-to-do girls. Functions. Guests. Julian among them. Julian might have been an unseen force behind Shirley's job of nursing his grandmother. A secret affair. Shirley installed in the family home, he assuring her: Let the family get to know you, and you'll see, it will be all right.

I can't marry him, I realize that now.

Why not? Because she realized, or had been compelled to acknowledge, that she was out of his class?

Class. Classy clothes. She had wanted to dress well to please her fiancé.

Sudden emotion deepened the creases around Bassett's eyes. Not much to ask from life, a few second-hand 'classy' clothes.

But Julian as the boyfriend didn't add up. According to Lisa, Shirley wouldn't break off the engagement because she didn't want to hurt the fiancé. She wouldn't have hurt Julian Pugh-Talbot, he had another fiancée lined up.

She hadn't wanted to hurt the boyfriend, he mulled on. For six months she hadn't wanted to hurt him. Six months.

Suggested a man whose heart she might break. A sensitive man . . .

Such a man came to mind. Tom Johnson, the teacher who had suffered a nervous breakdown. Might he have been, say, a patient at a hospital Shirley worked in during the school holidays? *I think he was sweet on her on the quiet . . . I found him crying* . . . Mrs Blest had said. She had also pointed out that Tom Johnson was twice Shirley's age.

A *father* figure? Might this explain the shame, call it discomfort? Pretty little gel Shirley—and a man nearly twice her age?

Bassett sighed, and went to keep his date with Andy.

Lisa watched the Citroën drive off, then she picked up the receiver and dialled.

'Angela? He's gone. Sat outside in his car for yonks. I daren't phone in case he came back.'

'What do you think?'

'I think you're right, Julian is a suspect. He said he's trying to clear their names. Does that mean they didn't kill themselves? I suppose it does.'

'We're going to have to tell the police, Lisa. It's all very well not wanting to get involved, but we know what happened, Shirley told us.'

'We don't know it's true—' Doubting Lisa.

'Does it matter? There's no law we can't repeat what Shirley told us.'

'What does Debbie say?'

'She couldn't hear everything he said to Mrs Pugh-Talbot but she got the distinct impression he wasn't there just to tie up loose ends. She says Mrs P-T looked worried sick and the minute he'd gone she put a call through to Julian. We *have* to speak up, Lisa.'

'All right. Look, I'll drop in on my way to work. Don't do anything till we've discussed it. See you.'

Lisa got all hot and fruitlessly busy again. 'I'll never get the house cleaned up in time. All go, go, go,' she complained to the cat. 'What's it to me if Shirley was raped!' A hand flew to her mouth. 'Oh, I shouldn't have said that! Shirley—forgive me!'

CHAPTER 14

Andy was waiting for Bassett outside their favourite town pub, an old coaching inn. 'I've warned Mabel we're coming. She's cooking steak and kidney and cottage pie.'

'I can smell both,' Bassett said, sniffing overtly.

Not for landlady Mabel the modern craze for container food and microwaves, she cooked the old-fashioned way and her customers loved her for it.

'I said we'd eat outside,' Andy said.

'Why not? Sun's shining.'

Mabel called out as they approached the side door. 'The usual, gentlemen?' The usual, please, they replied. Their pints of old ale were drawn by the time they got to the door. 'Steak and kidney or cottage pie?' Mabel said.

'Cottage pie. Same for you, Andy? Make that two, Mabel. Say in ten minutes' time.'

At the table: 'Mouth's watering,' Bassett said. Andy grinned and spread out a road map. 'Julian Pugh-Talbot. In his original statement he said he'd driven from Oxford, stopping off at the Black Swan for an hour, guvnor. It checked out OK until my fine-tooth combing picked up the direction he came from.' He traced the route on the map. 'From Oxford he'd have come Cheltenham, Gloucester, or—see—Tewkesbury. The A417 Or 438. He didn't—he came in on the B4214, look. The opposite direction. The direction he would have taken if he'd come from Briony House.'

He folded the map. 'I went to the Black Swan, then to see a few of their regulars, and came up trumps. Seems he passed the pub heading for home, returned fifteen minutes later, *then* he stayed till eight. Phoned his girl from the pub, overheard saying he'd be late, his mother had urgent business to discuss.

'He came into the station this morning, looking for you, matter of fact, sent by his mother. I said I didn't know why you wanted him, but I'd found a discrepancy needed straightening out. He was puzzled, couldn't understand why his doings on Friday night should have anything to do with the deaths on Saturday, but he'd answer the question. He said he drove past the pub in a dream, woke up and turned round. When I pointed out that wouldn't have cost more than a few minutes, he said he stopped and fiddled with his car stereo.'

'Why bother, if he was going to the pub?'

Andy nodded. 'Got it in one. In the end he admitted he'd gone home, was met by his mother in tight-lipped mood, so he turned round, back to the pub, timing his second arrival home to coincide with that of his pa.

'I asked him about the phone call. Didn't deny it, said the urgent business was *her* business—and his since he'd become a director. Refused to enlarge. In fact he made three calls, two with no reply. All he'd say about the two duds was that as he'd time on his hands he phoned a pal, who was out. It was pretty vague, but we can have another go at him. Specially now I've had a think.'

He smiled wryly. 'Thought I'd got something when I spotted he'd gone to the Black Swan from the direction of home. Didn't know he'd gone past from the right direction fifteen minutes earlier. Still queer, though.'

He drank some beer. Went on, 'He went home. Why lie

about it originally? Why did I have to drag it out of him this morning? Met by a tight-lipped mother, he says—so he high-tailed it to the pub. Why the pub? Then there's the phone call: his ma had urgent business to discuss. When did she tell him that? When she met him, tight-lipped?'

'And if it was urgent, why not discuss it there and then?' Bassett finished for him. 'That expression—tight-lipped. His or yours?'

'His,' Andy said.

'An expression a child might use. Children can be cruelly honest. *My mother was tight-lipped—*' Bassett imitated a small child. 'You can picture a mother looking extremely displeased about something. Or someone.'

'The rest of his answers aren't so innocent, guvnor.'

'Because things *happened* after that.' Bassett knew what he meant even if Andy didn't. By way of some explanation he continued, 'I gave his mother a message, told her I wanted to see him. She couldn't *not* pass it on, but I fancy she talked to him first.'

'Family conspiracy?' Andy ventured.

'Family!' Bassett exclaimed. 'I'm beginning to think everybody who knew Shirley is in it.' He told Andy about Angela and Lisa; and their jumping to Julian's defence.

Again Andy's smile was wry. 'You know what, guvnor? I've just strengthened his alibi. He couldn't have been haring off to the Black Swan *and* driving that car to the beauty spot. Lets him off the hook.'

'For murder,' Bassett said. 'Paternity? Now you've met him what are your impressions?'

'Have to admit I liked him.'

'No two-timer?'

'Wouldn't have thought so. Although, a one-off . . . A one-night stand, so to speak. A mistake . . . He's off the murder hook. Is his mother more firmly on it? If she didn't want him there, *ordered* him to clear off for an hour—'

'To a public house full of witnesses—'

'Question-mark against his father, too,' Andy went on. 'I told you Bob had a lead on Shirley's mother? He tracked her down to London. Couldn't get to talk to her, she's in hospital, cancer ward, terminally ill. Decided he might as well check up on Mr Pugh-T. His offices are in London, as you know. Seems Mr has no firm alibi for last Friday evening after all.

'We were originally concerned about the time he got home, if you remember. We hadn't worked round to thinking about an alibi; apparently neither had he. He'd said he left London between six-thirty and seven p.m., his office would bear him out. When it came to the crunch his office couldn't, except to verify that half past six to seven was the time he usually left, after the main exodus, motorways a lot less busy by then.

'His Friday routine seldom varied. Out in the morning to a meeting—lunch—couple of hours' shopping plus a trip to the barber's—back to the office, where he always worked late, everybody else going by four-thirty. Only difference last Friday was the morning meeting—with his bank, therefore he didn't take his secretary with him. Otherwise it was everything as usual. But no one is able to vouch for his whereabouts after he left the barber at half past two. It was assumed he would have followed the pattern and left at his normal time.

'Bob did manage five minutes with him. He said that as far as he was concerned last Friday was as any other. Why try to find an alibi when he hadn't known he would be required to provide one? Words to that effect.

'One more titbit. Shirley visited Mr's office last month, August. First time she'd done so to anyone's knowledge; valid reason—she was on her way to see her mother and her car broke down; within striking distance of Mr's office, apparently. He didn't take her, he laid a car on for her.

But—August. She would at least have had some suspicion that she was pregnant. With me?'

'With you, Andy.'

Anyhow, Bob was working on it, Andy said. 'Expecting a call from him at around two o'clock, guvnor.' He opened his notebook. 'Info scribbled every which way. Can't read my own hieroglyphics. What's this? Oh yes. From Doc. Conception July.' He looked up. 'I asked Julian about holidays—to find out if he and his father had been available, shall we say, in July. They had.

'Uncle Bertie—his story holds. No mistake, it was the old lady's birthday. She had neighbours in. Showed me a Polaroid snap of Bertie helping her to cut the cake. Both neighbours confirm that it was after half six when Bertie took his leave. So he would have got to Briony House at around seven-fifteen.'

Andy pocketed the notebook. 'Last entry, Miss Fletcher. Not a typical maid-of-all-work. One of the forgotten band of women who give up everything including a good job to look after ageing parents, was how the old lady described her. Although in the next breath she was having a go, saying she couldn't understand the woman. What it amounted to was that when the parents died Uncle Bertie urged Helen to follow her dream and go off and see the world for a year or two, she had earned it, could afford it, no longer had any ties—but she didn't, she took the job Mrs Pugh-T offered her.'

'She could afford to travel, you say?'

'Apparently. The parents left her comfortably off.'

'Any hint of an attraction keeping her at home? Tom Johnson?'

'None. There was a time—years ago. But nothing came of it. The old lady thinks Helen lost her nerve about the travelling, and took the Pugh-Talbot job for something to do. She doesn't really need to work, but housekeeping is something she can do with her eyes shut. And she's her own boss, more or less.'

'Makes sense to me. What doesn't the old lady understand about the woman?'

Andy grinned. 'Envy, I think, guvnor. The old lady would give anything to see the world, she's always been keen to travel, but has never had the wherewithal, and Helen—'

'Has cash and opportunity—going to waste, I suppose is how the old lady sees it.'

'Something like that, guvnor.'

Mabel called from the doorway: 'Cottage pies, piping hot! Ready, gentlemen?'

'Ready, Mabel!'

Andy stood up. 'What we need is a breakthrough.'

'What we need,' Bassett said, 'is the boyfriend.'

Both, in a manner of speaking, would be waiting for them when they returned to the station.

CHAPTER 15

The desk sergeant met them with: 'Young lady waiting for you. She's with Beattie in the canteen. Mrs Dee Harte. Used to work with Shirley Hughes at a school. She's a bit tearful.' He was a soft-hearted man.

'You go fetch her then, Tom. Cheer her up. We'll be in Bob Greenaway's office.'

Clearly Dee Harte had been made to laugh. Although her eyes were puffy from weeping, remnants of a smile had brightened her face. She looked to be in her mid-twenties; wore a predominantly salmon pink floral dress and jacket; and her long hair was tied back with a velvet bow.

'Hello. Come in! I'm Sergeant Miller, this is—'

'Bassett. Good to meet you, Mrs Harte.'

'Hello . . . Hello. Thank you.' As she sat down.

She cleared her throat. 'I've come about Shirley. What a dreadful shock!'

Her husband away on a computer course, she had decided to spend a day with friends in Hereford, she said. 'But they weren't pleased to see me, they had the builders in. So I thought I'd look Shirley up instead. What a shock when I got there! Mrs—Mrs Blest, is it?—the cook—?'

'Mrs Blest, yes.'

'She was so kind. I talked her head off. It was she who told me to come here. And now I am here I don't know what to say.'

'Why not say whatever comes into your head. Help us build up a picture of Shirley. We didn't know her, you see.'

Dee Harte nodded. 'She was nice. A bit uppity at first. We found out that was shyness.'

Bassett said: 'May I interrupt? Who are "we"?'

'We girls.' The domestic staff at Oakdean. 'Not all girls, of course, Joan and Millie are grandmas.' There were six of them altogether, Dee explained; they did the cooking, cleaning and dining-room duties.

Into this happy band of workers had come Shirley, who hadn't at first approved of their banter. 'Little Miss Prim and Proper! Credit where due, though, she was a good little worker.'

Another reminiscence, then: 'She used to watch the mistresses and pupils, studying them.' Dee giggled. 'She said some funny things when she first came. If she saw or heard anything she considered unladylike she'd say: I don't think that's breeding behaviour, do you? We had to get her to change the wording to "the behaviour of the well-bred" or something similar. She saw the funny side. Anyway she took it all in, spoke really nicely when she left. And she was smartly dressed. I overheard one of the mistresses saying one day: That girl is wasted here.'

And so to the boyfriend, the reason for Mrs Blest's suggesting Dee came to the station. 'It's probably not much use now, Shirley left Oakdean nearly two years ago, but she did have a boyfriend.

'About six months before she left Oakdean she came and asked me in a whisper if I'd look her over, to see if she passed muster to go out on a date. A date! My! I did wonder where she could have met him, she'd go for a walk in the day but the only time she went out at night was with us, or to one of our homes. Anyway, I said yes.

'Well! I'll never forget it! I don't think she'd used make-up in her life; didn't need to, to be honest, she was an English rose. And whoever sold her the stuff deserved a smacked bottom. Poor Shirley had piled it on—eye liner, eye shadow, rouge—and the lipstick! Purple! She looked like a sad clown. How I stopped myself from laughing I'll never know, poor kid.

'I asked her if she'd been wearing make-up when she met him. The first time, I meant. She said no. There you are, I said. He likes you as you are. If I were you I'd clean it off and start again, the art of applying make-up is to make it look as if you're not wearing any.

'I re-did her, and off she went. She was beautiful. All starry-eyed. Her first date—and she was very nearly eighteen!' A little starry-eyed herself as she spoke.

A short pause, a change of mood. 'The weeks went by, she had several dates, but never said much about the man. We never let on, but we began to think there wasn't one. We others were forever rabbiting on about our men, Millie's granddaughter was getting married and we were full of *her* preparations; we thought Shirley had invented an admirer so as not to be left out.'

But then, said Dee, came a day when she—Dee—was

in a teasing frame of mind. 'I pulled her leg. I saw you! I said. Last night! I saw you getting into a posh car!

'Honestly, she was worried silly. Begged me not to tell anybody. She got so worked up I had to tell her I'd been leg-pulling. The trouble was she had *me* worried after that. Who on earth was she going out with?

'I wondered if one of the pupils' fathers had given her the eye, or spun a tale. One's a film director, there *was* a photographer, glamour pics and that. And Shirley was so unworldly . . . Anyway, I had a private chat with her, AIDS and what-not. Offended her, poor kid. Nothing like *that* went on; they just drove to a place he knew, had a dinner and talked. He liked her for herself, she said, because she was different from other girls he'd taken out.'

'Did you ever find out who he was?' Andy asked.

Dee shook her head. 'No.'

Bassett: 'She never said much about him, you said. What *did* she say, can you remember?'

'He was tall, dark, and handsome. A gentleman. In Shirley's case that would mean, well, my husband is a gentleman, but he's ordinary. Shirley's *gentleman*—she'd mean—'

'Well-born?'

'Well-born, yes.'

'Anything else?'

'His car *was* posh. A BMW. The meals they had were—well, she ate food she'd never seen the like of. Lobster in its shell, asparagus . . . Doesn't sound like her Father Lambert, does it?' Dee wrinkled her nose.

'Mind you,' she said, 'Father Lambert was tall, dark, and handsome, and I suppose priests can have money tucked away. He might have enjoyed breaking free now and then and whooping it up. Shirley did begin to worry about the amount he spent on meals . . . But a BMW?'

Highly unlikely.

'No idea where the man took her to?'

None, Dee said.

'Did the name Pugh-Talbot crop up before Shirley left Oakdean?' Andy inquired.

Answer: No. 'She'd been left two months before I had a letter telling me she had moved again. She worked in a hospice, St Mary's, in between.'

The telephone rang. A few seconds later Andy voiced his apologies and left the room.

Bassett smiled at Dee Harte. 'We'll continue. Do the initials F.P. mean anything to you?'

'Fiona Paxley. Felicity Pugh. But they are girls. I can't think of anyone else.' She carried on thinking. 'Shirley bought a Mini from one of the senior girls. After she left Oakdean, when she was at the hospice. She wrote to me about it. Thrilled to bits and trying not to feel guilty—someone had told her the Mini was worth a whole lot more than she paid for it. No. I remember now—she bought it from Tessa Palmer.'

T not F—but P for Palmer clicked inside Bassett's head. Had Tessa a brother?

'A bargain she could afford,' he said, probing.

'Easily. Her gran left her five thousand in her will. I saw the cheque and solicitor's letter, they came before Shirley left Oakdean. She was so excited, she hadn't known she had a gran. Of course when it dawned on her that a will meant her gran had passed away she was sad, wished she had met her . . . She had her head screwed on. Apart from a car, she was going to buy clothes, and bank the rest. The Mini only cost a few hundred, I'm sure. As for the cheque! I can see her now, dancing for joy. She would never be poor again! The money would buy her a future!'

A further question had arisen: Who taught Shirley to drive? Dee couldn't help. All she knew—from letters—was that Shirley had passed her test while at the hospice.

Dee said it: 'I can't imagine a driving instructor with a BMW, can you?'

Bassett could not. He noted her address and telephone number, then: 'If you'll excuse me a moment.' Returning, he conveyed Sergeant Miller's thanks. Dee had cheered up considerably. She turned down an offer of more refreshment. 'I think I'll have a tour round Glevebourne. It looks a lovely little town.

'I dare say someone at Oakdean could tell you about the Mini,' she said as Bassett escorted her out. 'I left not long after Shirley.' And so missed in-house gossip.

Bassett thanked her. If he had read Andy's attempts at mime while he clutched the telephone to an ear, Bob Greenaway already had it.

Andy Miller was quietly excited. 'Bob's got the info Mrs Harte has just given us, only more of it.' Andy had listed the items. He enlarged as he went along.

One, Shirley's money was her own. £5000 bequeathed by her maternal grandmother. Unless her bank books, when found, showed a balance out of proportion, they could say she hadn't been subsidised by a lover.

Two, she had bought the Mini out of her legacy. As a matter of interest, one of her foster homes was a farm. The farmer's sons had all learnt to drive by the age of twelve. Unbeknownst to the foster parents, they maintained, the lads had taught Shirley, who had a natural aptitude. Hence the speed, after six official lessons, with which she had passed her driving test.

None of the lads had kept in touch with Shirley.

Three, Shirley had bought the Mini from a girl pupil at Oakdean, for a song. Rumour had it that the girl's folks were furious about the transaction, since the Mini was a collector's item inherited from the girl's aunt.

Four—'The big one, guvnor. Gen on a man Shirley was

friendly with while she was at Oakdean.' He grinned. 'Before you ask how Bob managed to do London and Oakdean in so short a time, I'll tell you—he enlisted the help of a local bobby for Oakdean. Chap calls daily—some trouble with a Peeping Tom a month ago. He's on tea and bun terms with domestic staff—one of whom told him she had seen the girl with *the brother* of one of the senior pupils. Whet your appetite?'

Bassett fed him a look.

'The woman kept it to herself till now. No particular reason, although she had warned Shirley at the time to be careful, the relationship would be frowned upon if she were found out. Shirley assured her that they knew to be careful.'

So careful she hadn't told her friend, Dee Harte.

'The girl's name is Tessa Palmer,' Andy said. 'Has a brother, Philip. P.P. not F.P. The local chap dug deeper and came up with Philip Frederick. Family insist on Philip—to old chums, and maybe Shirley, he was Freddie.'

'Freddie Palmer.'

'Ring a bell, guvnor? Society jewel thief? Two-day wonder in the press a couple of years back. Followed the Dream in the 'eighties, made his million, lost it when the bubble burst, and turned to thieving. Might have got away with it if he'd quit while he was winning, but they seldom do. Success made him more daring, he made a mistake, was caught red-handed. Some say by erstwhile friends who set a trap. Was tried and convicted a month after Shirley left Oakdean. She was then working in a hospice.'

And having driving lessons.

In the Mini supposedly bought from his sister Tessa.

'It's thought Tessa sold the Mini in a panic, she was raising cash everywhere—to help Freddie do a runner. Which he didn't. He thought, on advice received, he'd get probation. Shock of his life when he was sent down. He has to be the mystery boyfriend, guvnor. Not abroad—in prison.'

'And Shirley was afraid to wear his ring in case it was stolen property. She loved him, or thought she loved him; realized as time wore on that she had fallen out of love, and so could never marry him.'

'It fits.'

'It fits,' Bassett agreed. 'When did he come out? I take it he is out. There's a look on your face tells me the punch line is still to come.'

'He was released from gaol at the end of June.'

'Where is he now? Do we know?'

Bob was on it now, Andy said. 'Shouldn't take long to find out where he's *supposed* to be. He's going to phone back. Best wait for his call. What we need is something to place him within striking distance.'

Their lucky day! Bob Greenaway's call and a message from the front desk coincided. Bassett took the desk. That is he went down to meet a Mr Turnbull, who wanted to speak to somebody about 'the priest and the lass, Shirley Hughes'.

'I don't know if what I've got to say will be any help but there's been some talk about the priest and the young lass from Briony House, so I thought I'd best come.'

Albert Turnbull, grey-haired, ruddy-complexioned, hands calloused from heavy work, kicked off nervously as Bassett was showing him into an interview room.

'Sorry it's a bit stark in here, Mr Turnbull. I'm afraid I've nowhere more comfortable to take you,' Bassett said. 'It's good of you to come if you have information.'

'What it boils down to is this,' Albert Turnbull went on when they were seated. 'My granddaughter Tammy and her husband rent the lodge belonging to Briony House, and they told one of your constables they were out last Friday.

I reckon they were. What they didn't know till I told them was that I was at the lodge that evening.

'Trying to lick their garden into shape, they are, but with them both working and the nights drawing in now they don't get much of a chance. So after tea, nowt else to do, I went to give 'em an hour. Thought if I shifted a bit of undergrowth it would be something. I know where their tools are, so no bother there.

'Be about ten past six when I got to the lodge, and I hadn't been there about five minutes when this car parks itself. Red Maestro. 234 in the registration number, I can't recollect the rest. Comes and parks on what he'd've thought was wasteland.' In reality the proposed site of a garden pond. 'No fencing there, just levelled ground with piles of old bricks and bonfire stuff lying around.

'A youngish fella gets out of the Maestro and walks off up the drive towards the house. A stranger to me. I can't tell you how long he stayed either, I called it a day after the priest and the lass went past. The Maestro was still there.'

'Did he speak to you?' Bassett asked.

'Didn't see me. I'd gone round the corner to answer a call of nature. If I'd been quicker I'd've let him know he was on private property. But I didn't see him straight off, I only heard him. Silencer blowing. Hell of a racket it was making. He'll have had to have a new one fitted, the row t'other was kicking up no bandage would have fixed it.'

'Can you describe the man, Mr Turnbull?'

'Tall. Dark hair. Smartly dressed. Grey suit and collar and tie. In his twenties I should say.'

'Was he carrying anything?'

This required some thought. 'No. I leaned back to see who it was, saw him lock the car, put the keys in his pocket. He was wearing gloves. That's right, he was wearing gloves. But he wasn't carrying anything.'

'How did he look? Happy? Sad? Furtive?'

Albert Turnbull suddenly looked embarrassed. 'Now I think about it I've probably been wasting your time. He'd hardly be the picture of happiness, would he, silencer gone? He'd have been going to phone a garage. Haven't thought of that till now. If he'd waited he could've used the one at the lodge. Probably thought there was no one in, no light on anywhere. Ar, that's what it will have been—he went to Briony House to phone the garage.'

'He didn't though, did he?' Andy Miller said, Bassett having recounted what Arthur Turnbull told him. 'That's our man, guvnor. Released from gaol end of June. Friend of a friend let him have a cottage, also use of a red Maestro.

'Guess where the cottage is? On the Tewkesbury road, not a stone's throw away from here.'

CHAPTER 16

The cottage, tiny but well-cared for, standing in its own small plot of land, was aptly named The Retreat. The red Maestro stood in an open-fronted garage. Shirts, shorts, socks, were blowing on a line. From the half-open door to a scullery-type kitchen, the lingering scent of hot suds. The man who came to the door in response to Andy's knock answered the description of Freddie Palmer: tall, dark, handsome to some; well-spoken; confident.

Yes, he was Freddie Palmer, he said. Who were they? Arrogant. He was shaving, carried on shaving after asking them in. He was stripped to the waist: his stay in prison hadn't damaged a fine physique.

'You'll have to make it snappy, I have an appointment,' he said round the safety razor.

'Is that your Maestro outside?' Andy Miller said.

'Mine for the use of, yes.'

'New silencer.'

'They do wear out.' Freddie Palmer rinsed razor and brush under a tap. 'Every two years or so unless you buy stainless steel.' He bent over the sink, splashed his face free of lather and with one eye closed as if soap stung, reached for a towel. 'Why don't you stop beating about the bush and tell me what this is about?'

'That Maestro was seen at six-fifteen p.m. last Friday outside the lodge on the main drive to Briony House.'

'What a mouthful!' Mocking smile. 'Guilty as charged. Who bellyached?'

'Nobody. The person who saw you says you then went on up the drive towards the house.'

'So?' He finished towelling himself, took a freshly ironed shirt off a hanger on the back of a door.

'He assumed you were going to phone a garage.'

'And what do you think?' Fastening shirt buttons.

'Travelling from here you would have passed two public telephones. In any case you are only ten minutes away from Glevebourne.'

'Where there are garages and an Exhaust Centre.' His look mocked: Aren't you clever! 'Matter of fact the exhaust had been blowing for a day or two. The bloody thing went completely as I got to the drive. Bracket gone. Damn pipe was hanging off. I saw a place to park and used it.'

'But you didn't phone a garage from the house.'

'Who said I did?'

'Shall we stop playing games, Mr Palmer?' Andy's tone was abrupt. 'You were on your way to the house anyway, to see Shirley Hughes.'

'So?'

'Why didn't you phone from her flat?'

'Didn't go into the flat. Couldn't raise her.'

'So what did you do?'

'Her car was there, I thought she had gone for a walk. I hadn't passed her so I headed in the opposite direction.'

'Anyone see you?'

'How the hell do I know? I'd have sworn nobody saw me park on waste ground, but someone did. Might have been a bird watcher behind every tree—'

'Mr Palmer,' Bassett interrupted. 'You would do well to drop the levity. This is a murder investigation.'

'A what?' The fingers knotting the tie froze.

'Shirley didn't take her own life, she was murdered.'

'Oh Christ!' Freddie Palmer turned away from them, tie forgotten, hands clenched at his sides. A few minutes, and he turned, distraught, and pointed. 'In here.' He led them into the next room, where there were chairs, and a bottle of whisky. 'Mind if I have a drink?'

'When you are ready,' Andy said, 'perhaps you would tell us about your relationship with Shirley.'

'It was over.'

'I mean from the beginning. Where did you meet her?'

'At Oakdean, my sister's school.' He looked forlornly from Andy to Bassett and back again. 'You know that. I've no doubt you'll have done your homework.'

'We'd still like to hear your version, Mr Palmer.'

'I'm a suspect? Hell, what a mess!' He wiped a hand over his face, gripped his mouth. 'How did I meet Shirley? It was at one of those end-of-term fund-raising parties Oakdean is famous for . . .'

His sister Tessa used to bully him into going, he said; she liked to show him off to her friends; having an eligible bachelor brother increased her popularity. He was happy to humour Tessa; why not? On this particular occasion, though, he wasn't in the mood for her giggly schoolpals. He was in trouble, trying desperately to keep it from the parents—even hoping the charges would be dropped. 'I was ready to plead insanity, *any*thing,' he said with fervour.

'Still, I went to this party thing for Tessa's sake. Tried not to show that her friends irritated me. Suddenly, there was Shirley, sweet, kind, soft-spoken, shy; an aura of untouchability about her. Vastly different from other girls I knew, and very refreshing, I can tell you.

'I asked her out three times before she said yes. I'd no idea who she was, and by the time I found out I frankly didn't give a damn, I was crazy about her.

'She was great to be with. Calm, gentle, undemanding, and no dumb blonde, she was very intelligent. I only got her to come out with me in the end by promising there would be no strings attached. I needed her—to talk to. That is all we ever did: walk, talk, eat and laugh.'

'You proposed marriage to her eventually.'

'I needed her. When my trial loomed I told her what I had done. I needed her quiet strength, not with me in court, but behind the scenes.'

'She didn't go to the trial?' Bassett's question.

'No, I got her to promise not to. Press out in force, cameras flashing, I'd have been a laughing-stock.'

He didn't see Bassett's eyes narrow.

'I honestly never thought I'd go to prison, but in case the worst should happen I asked her to write to me. She did. Incredible. She wrote every week. I never did write back, but occasionally we would speak on the phone, I was allowed to do that.'

'Why did you never write? Was it your idea to keep your relationship a secret?'

A shrug. 'It just came about. There was I—a villain, and there was Shirley. Who was to know if she might meet someone else? Which she did, obviously.'

'She wrote and told you?' said Andy.

'She wasn't the type to send a Dear John. No. I detected a cooling off towards the end of my sentence. I won't pretend I was worried; if I'm honest I was relieved. I had almost forgotten what she looked like. I decided to make it easy for her: instead of rushing to a phone when I got out I waited a few days. Then I let another week pass while I sorted a few things out and moved in here.'

Only then did they meet: one summer evening at a pub on the banks of the River Severn.

'I nearly fell for her a second time. She had become sophisticated, self-assured. Still kind, though, the same sweet Shirley underneath. I couldn't really tell how she felt about me; we were both shy, like two people on a blind date. We saw each other three times in all—' He broke off, overcome with emotion.

'She told me about her studies, her ambitions,' he continued. 'I thought *she* was trying to let *me* down lightly. Which I preferred. I wanted her to do the breaking-off.'

'Why?' Bassett said tersely.

'In case I was wrong.'

'Did she do the breaking-off?'

'I can't remember which of us did. One night we both started off as normal, by the end of the main course we had agreed to call it quits.'

'When was this?'

'Weeks ago. I told you, I only saw her three times.'

'It is now September,' Andy said. 'What was last Friday all about?'

'To collect a ring. I gave her a ring before my trial.'

'Stolen property?'

'Actually it wasn't. Purchased with untainted money. A deal of money. You are now going to say she never wore it. I know, she told me. She thought it was stolen. Why did it take me so long to go and ask for it back? I went to stay with my folks, spent my days riding, sleeping, eating—in other words, recuperating. Prison's no fun.'

'Where is the ring now?'

'I was going to ask you.'

'Shirley didn't give it back?'

'She wasn't there, I told you.'

'Ah yes. You thought Shirley had gone for a walk, and you went looking for her. Try the flat later?'

'No, I did not—'

'The Maestro was still there at seven-thirty.'

'If you'll let me finish. I carried on walking, got a lift the last mile to Glevebourne, in the hopes of finding somewhere open. I did. Receipt in that drawer. I bought a system, begged a length of string, took a taxi; tied the existing pipe on with the string, limped back here, and put the new system on the next morning. Taxi-driver's name is Alec. The chap at the exhaust centre let me use his phone. He—Alec—was out on a call. I waited for him to pick me up by the market hall, which he did at ten past eight.'

'So you didn't see Shirley at all?'

'No. I phoned on Saturday morning. No reply. The rest of the day was taken up with fitting the new exhaust system. Saturday night I went to the pub up the road, and heard them talking. It made me feel ill until I heard them say the girl was pregnant. Then I felt better, it wouldn't have been Shirley. But it was. I remember thinking that she was so good the only man she *would* have allowed near her would be a bloody priest.'

There was a short heavy silence.

Then Bassett said evenly, 'If we could borrow that receipt, Mr Palmer.' And, taking the slip of paper, 'You say you never entered Shirley's flat on Friday. Had you ever been there?'

'Once, when she drank too much wine. I drove her home.'

'She wasn't accustomed to drink? No. Was she noisy, tiddly?' Shaking his head as Freddie Palmer shook his. 'Did she fetch her car next day or did you deliver it?'

Freddie Palmer seemed not to like the question.

'I ask,' Bassett said, smiling, 'because Shirley does seem to have kept you a close secret. If she hadn't died, I doubt if anyone would have known about you.'

Did Shirley's ex-fiancé see, as Andy Miller saw, the expression behind Bassett's eyes? Perhaps. Perhaps when he gazed down at his glass it was to hide the sudden fear in his own. Perhaps when he tossed the whisky down it was to give himself Dutch courage.

'We had to meet in secret when she was at Oakdean, her job would have been in jeopardy. Through the trial—I was protecting her. Afterwards, her career. It wouldn't have done her a lot of good if word had got out that her boyfriend was a gaolbird, would it?'

'I don't suppose it would, Mr Palmer. Is that it for now, Sergeant Miller?'

'I think so. We may need to speak to you again, Mr Palmer. You'll be here?'

'For a week or two.'

'Shirley's Mini,' Bassett said, as they went through the kitchen. 'Worth a bob or two, they say. Considerably more than she paid your sister for it—mm?'

'Not so valuable now. She's clocked up some miles. Tessa always was impulsive, she had a crackbrained notion about smuggling me out of the country. Could I buy it back from Shirley's estate?' Mockery there again. 'I'd like to make Tessa a present of it.'

'Good day, Mr Palmer.'

'Well?' Andy said, as they made for the lay-by where their car was parked.

'He said it himself: Guilty as charged.'

'He says he's never been inside the flat. What were you thinking of, guvnor? If we find a fingerprint?'

'You won't. He was wearing gloves. You just might find one in the Mini, though—where you wouldn't expect to find one. Obvious places are no good—a lawyer will tell you of a hundred ways they could have got there.'

'You're losing me,' Andy said. 'Hang on, I'm getting there. He never answered the question about whether he delivered or Shirley collected the Mini, did he?'

Bassett flashed him a doesn't-matter look. 'What is important is that he had it overnight. Where better than the Mini, in the tender care of Shirley, unconnected with the case, to stash some of his haul?'

'For nigh on two years?' Andy was dubious.

'He didn't know it would be that long, Andy. You heard him: he honestly didn't believe he'd go to prison. Shock of his life when he did, you said. Could be why he used to phone Shirley. Not to say I love you—to ensure she held on to the Mini. Dodgy in a letter, simple as part of a telephone conversation. The kind of thing you say when you can't think of anything else: Still got the Mini, love? Hang on to it. You won't get another like that in a hurry. Innocuous.

'He's cocksure the Mini is clean. He's scared all the same. Pulses throbbing where he never knew he had 'em,' Bassett rumbled. 'Prison, probably . . .'

Andy began a low laugh. 'Smacks of *Schoolboy's Own* when you think about it—precious stones stashed in a Mini.'

'And his character's out of a romantic novel,' Bassett said drily. 'Gentleman Jewel Thief. No smash and grab and swag bag for him. The dashing hero was his style. In evening dress, beautiful girl on his arm, stolen jewels in his pockets . . .'

'Dashing heroes don't commit murder, guvnor.'

Bassett grunted. Twice.

CHAPTER 17

Bassett had some thinking to do when he took his dog out later that afternoon. Not surprisingly, he dwelt first on the suspect interviewed last: Freddie Palmer.

His thoughts were random and those of a cynic.

I had no idea who she was . . . By the time I found out I was crazy about her . . .

Crazy about her? That is infatuation. Infatuation isn't love.

He had kept Shirley away from the trial; that is, he kept her out of the eye of the press. Not for her sake, for his own: *I'd have been a laughing stock.*

He had used the girl; had abused the very innocence that attracted him to her when he was badly in need of a comforter.

He had given Shirley a ring? Why? As an investment? Had he given it to her knowing full well he would one day get it back?

Thus began Bassett's thoughts. Yet he was naturally fair-minded. It was his fair-mindedness that nudged him in the ribs and whispered: Not that mercenary, surely.

Perhaps not, no. Perhaps he should start again, and take into consideration that what Freddie Palmer had said today was related to thoughts and feelings now.

Right-oh. A re-write. As things were two years ago. Thereby giving Freddie Palmer some benefit of doubt.

I had no idea who she was. By the time I found out I was crazy about her . . . Believe that to have been sincere at that time. But put it in the same category as a patient at low ebb who falls in love with his nurse. He had given Shirley a ring as a token of that love. Two years ago the ring was a gift. Two years ago he wouldn't have dreamed of asking for it back. *Now* he wants it. So long as it was bought honestly there would be a receipt somewhere. With a receipt Freddie could safely and openly raise cash on the ring. Was that why he was keen for Shirley to break off the engagement? 'Sorry, Freddie, I can't marry you, here is your ring . . .' If *he* had done the breaking off Shirley could have kept the ring by way of compensation. Did he need the ring? Need as in being short of cash? Why? How come he was in need of cash if there were stolen gems in the Mini? A Mini to which he'd had overnight access?

I waited a few days—when he got out. Then another week passed . . .

What did he do during that week? Where did he go?

He would have had an accomplice, Bassett reasoned. A fence. And two years *is* a long time. Shirley could have had an accident, could have traded in the Mini . . . Suppose an accomplice was to have retrieved the stolen goods. Suppose he did, before Shirley ever moved to Briony House. Suppose when Freddie went to collect his share of the loot the cupboard was bare.

Bassett toyed with the idea of Shirley having been more astute than given credit for; but discarded the idea. She knew when Freddie was due for release; if she robbed him, she wouldn't have hung around for him to find her.

Try another tack. Freddie admitted he went to see Shirley on Friday. On the face of it he had gone openly, in daylight; therefore he hadn't gone with the intention of killing her.

Wearing gloves. A woman might wear gloves in summer; would a man, for other than driving? A man like Palmer might, from habit, the habit of a thief. Perhaps he did go to get the ring—to steal it back if necessary; Shirley wasn't fussy about locking her door.

On the other hand, a month had gone by since they had seen each other . . . What if what Freddie Palmer said about his cooling off was bunkum? What if he did still love the girl, went to plead with her—and when he got there she told him she was carrying another man's baby?

If he had truly loved her, and she toppled off that pedestal he had put her on . . .

But wouldn't there be remorse afterwards? There was no remorse in Freddie Palmer; only self-love.

And fear. Oh yes, there had been fear.

Shirley. Bassett brought her alive in his mind's eye. A girl who wanted better than life had doled out to her, who seized the opportunity when it came, her grandmother's legacy, and used it wisely: a car for independence, good clothes for self-esteem, studies to improve her education. She sees a new life ahead; an exciting new life. A bright nineteen-year-old, head filled with dreams but feet firmly on the ground.

Then she ruins everything by getting pregnant.

Suddenly Bassett's mind was firing shots. The burglary in July. Shirley's pregnancy. Fear—fear of prison.

Presently he called to his dog. His face was the face the labrador knew well, kind and creased with smiles; his voice the same voice that could soothe fretful children and animals when no other could. There was nothing grating or harsh about Harry Bassett. For all that he was a big man—he had been called beefy in his time—he was quiet, co-ordinated, gentle. Only a close observer, a friend who knew him well, could have told you that inside this quiet man walking home with his dog there was deep sorrow and seething anger.

At home, he put a call through to the station.

'Andy, make a note. End of June—Palmer released from gaol. July—the Pugh-Talbots burgled. July again—Shirley conceives. I think they're connected.'

CHAPTER 18

He was going to have to get *really* tough, Bassett was thinking as he got his dog her tea, for it was to his own place he had returned after their walk. Young Angela from Phoenix Fashions knew more than she let on. Must know more. She said the ring could be stolen property, then looked as if she could have bitten her tongue out. Ha! They'd learn. Very few people could fool him for ever.

The telephone rang as he went to pick it up.

Mrs Pugh-Talbot. 'Oh good, I've got you at last, Mr Bassett. We were talking about Shirley's boyfriend. I regret having to say this, but I think you'll find it was our gardener, Mr Johnson. They have been seen out walking together.'

'Many people walk together, Mrs Pugh-Talbot.'

'Yes, it does sound absurd put like that. But they haven't been straight about it. Do you see? Secrecy.'

'He was tutoring her, surely, Maths and English.'

'Yes, he was. And there were occasions when Helen was with them, all three of them together. But there were also other times. Also, a wealthy boyfriend, you said. You will have seen Shirley's wardrobe, far more clothes than her salary would allow. My son doesn't have that sort of money to spare.'

'A gardener has?' Bassett said wisely.

A sigh came down the line. 'Mr Johnson inherited a considerable amount of money from his parents. Moreover, he spends little. He is not a poor man by any stretch of the imagination.'

'Forgive me, but surely if Mr Johnson and Shirley had been dating, under the same roof, so to speak, it would have been impossible to hide for long. Indeed, why should they want to hide their feelings for each other?'

'The age difference could come into it. He's twice Shirley's age. There is also Helen. They might have been sparing her feelings. It was taken for granted by many of us that when Helen was free—when she no longer had to look after her parents—she and Tommy—'

'Helen and Tommy had an understanding?'

'We used to think so, yes. Anyhow, I've given you the information. What you do with it is up to you.'

'One moment, Mrs Pugh-Talbot. What put you on to it?'

'Concern for my son, Mr Bassett. Julian seems to be coming in for a deal of attention. Undeserved, I will add. He has a brilliant future ahead of him. I will not stand by and let that future be harmed.'

End of call.

Receiver down; the telephone rang again. This one started out as a social call.

'Harry Bassett, you're devilish hard to catch these days. Working?'

'How did you guess!'

'Didn't. A little bird told Jack.' Jack Carter, or Jack the Poacher, friend of Bassett and Willy Brewerton. The caller was Jack's lovely wife, another Helen.

'Reason I'm phoning, Harry, I'm giving a small soirée to celebrate Jack's new book.'

'About Shire horses?'

'Yes. Comes out in a fortnight's time. You will come, won't you?'

'Wouldn't miss it for the world. Helen?' Helen bred labradors and horses. 'Do you know Eva Pugh-Talbot?'

'We've met. She no longer rides. The last time I actually spoke to her was, oh, three years ago, when she brought the live-in help she had then, nice girl, Pippa—Pippa

Grosvenor—to look round the riding school. Pippa was horse mad, wanted to book a few rides. It didn't last long, Pippa left Briony House soon afterwards.'

'Know why?'

'A more glamorous job. In Saudi Arabia. She'd only really been filling in for the Pugh-Talbots after their previous help retired. Got this super job. The people were flying out almost immediately and wanted Pippa to fly out with them. She left at a moment's notice.'

'You know that for a fact, Helen?'

Helen Carter made noises down the line; but with a smile in her voice. 'You want gossip.'

'A copper's lifeblood!'

She chuckled. 'Rupert, Eva's husband, was a mite free with his—attentions, shall we say? Nothing serious. Pippa found his attentions more amusing than annoying; she felt sorry for him, verbal games were played, all with a humour apparently never offensive. Affection was what he wanted, Pippa said; someone to hug him now and then.'

She paused. 'Harry—I'm not sticking up for the man, but I don't think he'd be such a fool as to play around on his own doorstep again.'

'Again?'

'Oh. I thought you'd heard.'

'Shan't mind hearing it a second time.'

'Rupert and a local woman a few years ago. Caused a stir. Apparently Uncle Bertie put an end to it; he read Rupert the riot act, advised him to get a pretty trollop in Town. Better that than break up the happy home.'

'And Eva is aware of this. Right?'

'Aware. Accepts. Not that she would admit it to you. Or me. Quite rightly. Not so long as they remain a devoted couple in public. They do *like* each other, oddly enough. For them the arrangement works. Any help?'

'Big help, Helen. Thanks.'

'Any time.' They rang off.

Angela from Phoenix Fashions made a third caller. She came on the telephone while Bassett was looking up her number. She sounded nervous.

'I hope you don't mind my phoning. You're not in the middle of tea or anything?'

'No, I'm alone with my dog, wondering what to do with myself,' Bassett fibbed. 'What can I do for you?'

'We'd like to see you, Lisa, Debbie and me. There's something we think you ought to know.'

'Can't you tell me now on the phone?'

'No, it needs all three of us.'

'Where shall we meet?'

'We thought the shop. Debbie can't get here until eight o'clock. Would that be convenient?'

Bassett said it would.

At Glevebourne Police Station Andy Miller had just finished speaking to Bob Greenaway. Bob was on his way back. 'I'll go straight home, Andy, advise you to do the same, could be a busy day tomorrow.'

Andy took the Inspector at his word, hurriedly tidying the office first. Bob Greenaway's two-thirds of the office, that is. His own corner was a perpetual mess; he worked by the heap system, and was too old to change.

He stopped at the front desk before leaving. 'If Bassett comes or phones will you tell him Bob's on his way, we'll be in touch in the morning.'

He pulled his coat collar up against a cool night air, and danced down the steps to his waiting Joanna.

Bassett dropped his dog off at his neighbour's house on the way to Phoenix Fashions.

The shop was restfully lit, subtly perfumed as much by its daytime flow of customers as by the present three occupants, and was as warm as shops usually are when you are entering them straight off the street.

Debbie Shaw, Mrs Pugh-Talbot's secretary, was barely recognizable in jeans and a coat of many colours. Lisa—she of the long legs and gabby nature—was holding a skimpy black lace evening dress against herself and swinging her hips provocatively. 'Hi! Mr Bassett!' she called as she 'fitted' the strapless top to her sweatered bosom. Then she thrust hanger and dress at arm's length towards Angela. 'Don't sell this, I might go mad and buy it.'

Angela, whose hair in this light was titian, looked quite beautiful. In another age, Bassett thought, she might have been much in demand as an artist's model.

'We're a bit short of chairs,' she said awkwardly.

'Mr Bassett's not here for a tea-party, are you, Mr Bassett?' Forthright, irreverent Lisa promptly sat cross-legged on the floor. Debbie joined her. Bassett smiled at Angela: 'Problem solved.' He too lowered himself to sit on the floor. Oh yes, he was supple enough.

'I like you,' said Lisa. 'You're great.'

'What is it you want to tell me?' he said, addressing all three. They looked at one another, then began talking all at once.

'She—Shirley—in August it was—told us she was two weeks late—you know—and—'

They stopped.

Lisa the hard one cried. 'Poor Shirley. We let her down. *I* let her down. She needed us, and all I could do was make fun of her. I didn't *believe* her.'

Angela: 'You see, she told us she had been raped. We told her to go to the police, but she couldn't do that, she said, they'd . . . Well, it wasn't as if she had been attacked by a stranger, it would be her word against his.'

'She knew the man?' Bassett said. Rhetorically.

Debbie: 'I advised her to tell Mrs Pugh-Talbot, but Mrs Pugh-Talbot was the *last* person she wanted to tell.'

'Why was that?'

'Shame, I imagine.'

Lisa: 'We should have been better friends to her. It was my fault we weren't. I thought she was conning us all. If there *was* a boyfriend, and she wanted rid of him—well, a baby on the way was a perfect *out*, and she'd have us to back her up. He wouldn't be quite so hurt if we said she wasn't to blame, she'd been faithful all the time he was away, and so on, pleading her case—'

Debbie: 'Then when they were found—Shirley and the priest—we—we put two and two together. We thought: What a predicament! We thought Father Lambert must have been the mystery boyfriend and—'

Angela: 'And—well, if he wasn't going to leave the priesthood for her, and yet still, you know, went to bed with her—well, Shirley might have told herself, you know, that it was nothing short of rape.'

Lisa: 'I feel *rotten*. I never believed a word she said.'

'But now you do,' Bassett said.

They did. 'It wasn't Julian,' Debbie volunteered. 'For one thing he's a perfect gentleman. For another, we started remembering some of the things Shirley said—'

'Things that hadn't meant much before,' Lisa put in.

'—For example, when we asked her what she was going to do about it she said: I think I'll tell Julian and Pen, I've always been able to talk to them.'

'Are you telling me the truth?'

'Honestly,' they said. 'That's what she said.'

'Also,' said Angela, 'I remember her saying: What will Father Lambert think of me! And she wasn't saying it just to throw us off the scent, we've decided. She looked too distressed.'

The most important thing they had remembered, Debbie

said, was Shirley suddenly looking furious. She said: The Beast! What an idiot I've been! I've known all along he was a rotter!'

Honestly, they were telling the truth.

'Who do you *now* think she was referring to?' Bassett said.

'The boyfriend, whoever he is,' they said.

CHAPTER 19

'That's all very well, Harry, but Palmer wouldn't be such a fool as to lie about when he bought the exhaust system, and he couldn't have been doing that and haring round the countryside in the priest's car.'

'Fact,' Bassett murmured innocently.

It was the following morning. Bob Greenaway seemed to be in an argumentative mood; worse, a black mood, disposed to argue for argument's sake. Andy Miller kept out of it until Bob was called to another office, then he treated Bassett to a broad wink and an explanation.

'Couple of bods who worked on Palmer's original case are coming to take a look-see at the Mini. Might do themselves a bit of good if they come up with a lead to any of the missing loot. But Robert's none too pleased.'

Bassett saw the light. 'You mean he's not keen on me, his erstwhile gaffer, being here when they come. They might think he's being nursemaided. Has anyone managed to get to the Exhaust Centre, or shall I go?'

Andy had been himself. 'Found an old mate of mine working there. He remembered Palmer; a man calling himself Palmer. Description fits. Turned up not long after seven o'clock, miffed about having to miss out on the free-of-charge fitting, said he'd had to abandon his car, the pipe had fallen off. Sounds like him, right? We're going to make sure. We've asked Palmer to come in; we'll bend the rules a fraction: my mate will just happen to be working in the car park when he arrives. If our Freddie Palmer isn't the tall, dark-haired chap who bought a new exhaust system on Friday—if by chance that one was a tall, dark-haired chum of Palmer's—we've got him.'

'If not, as Bob rightly said, he couldn't have been in two places at once,' Bassett said philosophically. 'I'll make myself scarce for the rest of the day.'

He crooked a finger: 'Use your phone?'

He rang up his widowed lady friend. 'I'm available this morning after all, Grace. Be with you in half an hour to take you shopping.'

Leaving: 'Before I go. Andy—that walk Palmer says he went on, looking for Shirley. Ask him if he saw anyone. He was so busy being clever he forgot to tell us.'

'Took it remarkably well,' Andy told Bob Greenaway when the latter sneaked back. 'Didn't even pretend to be not offended. If you get me.'

That Andy passed on this information po-faced and tongue-in-cheek, if both are possible at one and the same time, was lost on Bob. Proof if ever it were needed that Andy knew Bassett better than Bob did. And it was Andy who in a quiet moment smiled secretively and asked himself: 'What's Bassett up to?' For as sure as he grew apples in his orchard Bassett was up to something.

For the remainder of the morning Bassett wasn't 'up' to anything. He took his friend shopping, his dog for a walk while Grace prepared an early lunch; but then, shortly after one o'clock, he set off again on his travels.

Uncle Bertie stood in the library at Briony House staring into space; more accurately staring down at the space between his feet. Whatever had got into Helen? He'd approached her pleasantly enough: 'Helen, I overheard you and Shirley last Friday morning . . .' and gracious me! the woman flared up as fast as a brush fire in a gale: 'When? Don't you go accusing me of anything! I know nothing! Nothing!'

Bertie was perplexed. What had he said? More to the point, what did Helen think he was going to say? He'd heard low voices, hadn't listened intentionally, was in a bit of a daze to tell the truth, and looking for the Grayling twins, who'd been brought in by Shirley after their dancing class. He'd heard only snatches: '. . . Morning sickness . . . bit peaky . . . can't keep it to yourself . . .' Girl talk as far as he knew. About some unfortunate gel and what in his day had used to be whispered about as 'a case'. Never entered his head that the gel might be Shirley until the tragedy, when to all intents and purposes it had appeared to slot into place.

Different now. The police were dissatisfied; so was he. Oh yes, so was he.

He moved ponderously from library to kitchen, where Mrs Blest informed him that Helen had gone home. Oh well, no matter. Couldn't make head or tail of it, but there it was. All he'd wanted to ask was had Shirley said, or had she intimated *who*.

'Come on, lads!' He took the dogs out.

Bassett parked at the front of Briony House and let himself into the garden by the side gate. He wanted Tommy Johnson, found only familiar fragrance and birdsong; and in due course the cook, Mrs Blest, whose face at sight of Bassett dropped irritably. 'Tommy? He's gone to Benn's Nurseries up the lane for supplies.' As if she had time to worry about Tom Johnson and his doings.

All of a which way the house was today; Helen dashing off in a huff, not that she was on duty, only hanging about in case she might miss something; Master Julian in and out; and Mrs Pugh-Talbot; Mr coming home a day early; everybody biting one another's head off. She'd have gone home herself if she hadn't promised to re-stock the freezer with pastries, she really would.

'And now you are grabbing a precious five minutes—' for the cook was sitting down to a cup of tea—'and in I walk!' Said so mournfully Mrs Blest had to laugh.

'Oh . . . sit yourself down, I'll get another cup. Have to have a moan now and then to prove I'm breathing.'

'Don't we all!' Bassett agreed.

'If it's urgent you could get Tommy on the phone,' Mrs Blest said helpfully, pouring his cuppa.

'I only wanted to pick his brains about a climbing plant for a north wall,' Bassett fibbed; continuing conversationally, 'How is he? Missing Shirley the last time I saw him, as I recall.'

'Yes, he will miss her, that's for sure. She brought him out of himself, in my opinion. A breath of fresh air, the girl was. Not as I see a lot of him, but I was thinking only this morning he'll have no one to spoil now.'

'Spoil?'

'She had her own kitchen in the flat, you see. Tommy would bring her a basket from his garden: lettuce, tomatoes, spring onions, potatoes . . . June and July there'd be soft fruits, raspberries and strawberries. Oh! Shirley and her strawberry jam! Made pounds of it! Off she'd trot to his place, he had the pots and pans left by his mother. Pounds and pounds, she'd make. He'll miss all that. And the fun, her companionship. She made him laugh.'

'He still has Helen.'

'Yes . . . I was thinking more of the teaching sessions. He did enjoy them. He'd probably never have had a nervous breakdown, he said, if all his pupils had been as eager to learn as Shirley. Yes, he'll miss her.'

'Helen didn't mind?'

'About Shirley? No. Why should she? She used to go as well sometimes.'

'Oh, I fancied Helen and Tommy—' Bassett gestured.

'I think their mothers lived in hopes, they had been childhood sweethearts. Maybe that was the trouble—they ended up knowing too much about each other, no mystery left. And if there's no love there, no use drifting into marriage, that way leads to misery. No, I think Tom's just not the marrying kind. Can't say I blame him, he's got a lovely home, plenty of money. No one to nag him,' she said with a laugh. 'Has its compensations, my hubby says.'

Presently Bassett inquired after Uncle Bertie.

'He'll have gone to Helen's, like as not, to patch up their quarrel.' She had no idea what the tiff was about, Mrs Blest said. One of those days, everybody at everybody else. 'If he's not with Helen, try John's lake, he likes to sit and contemplate the water.'

Where had been peace was not so peaceful when Bassett hit the top drive. Tommy was no longer at the nurseries, he was a distant figure riding a power mower at the far end of the front lawns. Bassett stood; considered. There, the man. There, the chimneys of his house. There, a hedge and a stile separating lawns from adjoining field . . . and what appeared to be a well-worn path across the field. Tommy's short cut?

One way to find out. Tommy must have spotted him by now. He set a course, climbed the stile, crossed the field.

Uncle Bertie was waiting for him when he reached the other, lane, side.

Bertie had opened the gate and was leaning on his stick when Bassett spurted to safety.

'Olé!' Bertie cried.

'See the size of him!' Bassett gasped, glancing over his

shoulder at the bull with a ring in its nose not far behind. They fastened the gate, shutting the bull in.

'A Hereford,' Bertie said. 'Docile as a lamb.'

'Still a big 'un!' said Bassett.

At which, Bertie's shoulders began to shake; both men snorted, and the dogs, two retrievers and a mongrel, became suspended for a second, statue still, watching two elderly men as they fell about laughing.

'Walk?' Bertie said, dabbing at his eyes.

'Surely.'

They crossed the lane to where verges were wider, wild flowers thicker beneath the hedges; the dogs could have fun exploring, and they could comfortably walk two abreast.

'Glad we've met,' Bertie said. 'Been troubled since our last meeting. Troubled before, mystery as to why. Not all clarity now. Blessed car, Friday evening. Took it for granted the priest was at the wheel, no cause to think anything else over the weekend. Now, I couldn't swear to it. Have to get it right, inquest coming up.'

With a long lean forefinger he prodded his brow. 'In here I see fair hair at the nape of the neck; fair or grey.'

He stared straight ahead, beard thrusting forward, then back as he chewed his teeth. Stared as if searching for better than a hazy image in his memory of the figure behind the wheel. 'The priest had dark hair.'

'Yes.'

'Black robe thing and hat on the back seat.'

'Yes.'

'Somebody else could've been wearing 'em.' The blue eyes were suddenly rheumy, not Bertie's at all.

'Who do we have?' Bassett said levelly. 'Julian is blond. His mother—'

'Tommy Johnson.' Bertie held the name aloft; dashed it to the ground. 'But Tommy doesn't drive.'

A silence fell.

Bassett said: 'How does he fetch nursery supplies?'

'Doesn't. Walks down to select his order. Either they deliver or Helen fetches them in the house van.'

A few more strides brought them to a sprawling house whose old-fashioned garden belonged in picture books.

'Tommy's,' Bertie said. 'Used to be two cottages and a barn; Tom's dad knocked them into one. Locally famous gardener in his day, spot on the wireless, wrote books. He and Tom's mother were killed in a car accident. Hit Tommy hard. Fog: Blasted stuff.'

'His breakdown?'

'Triggered it, I shouldn't wonder. Although teaching had been getting him down. Carried on to please his dad. Only temporary at Evie and Rupert's of course, while he gets himself together.'

To return to Friday. 'Mrs Pugh-Talbot recognized Father Lambert.' It came out as a question.

'Evie can't swear either. Asked me.'

'When did she ask you?'

'Saturday. Your colleagues wanted to know when we'd last seen young Shirley. I told 'em I'd seen her leaving with the priest, Evie said the same. Later Evie asked if I was certain it was Father Lambert, I'd been closer to the car than she had. Yes, I said, damn thing nearly knocked me for six!'

At this juncture Bertie halted, hooked his stick on a wrist, produced a cheroot case, and offered them.

Bassett declined: 'Pipe, thanks.'

'Might've been a trick of the light,' Bertie mumbled. 'Blessed car zig-zagging. Lamp on by the gatepost . . . Yes, might have been a trick of the light.'

'Did you see anyone in the grounds, then or later?'

With some deliberation Bertie slid the cheroot case back into his pocket. 'Tommy. Later, on my way out.' He lit the cheroot, resumed walking. 'Looking for Shirley. Neglected to say why. I told him she'd gone with her priest friend.'

'What was his reaction?'

'Couldn't say. Thanked me and tootled off.'

'Think he was sweet on Shirley, Bertie?'

'Man's a bookworm,' Bertie said at length. 'Bookworms are often romantics. They seek perfection. Occasionally they find it.'

The dogs had congregated near a public footpath sign some yards farther on. Bertie turned to Bassett. 'Waiting for my signal,' he said with a semblance of a grin. 'Won't go on till I give it.' He projected his cry: 'Good boys! That way! Lake's worth seeing, Bassett—'

Bassett was tempted, but no. 'Another time, perhaps. Enjoyed our chat.'

'And the bull, what!'

Bassett gripped the hand Uncle Bertie held out. He was to remember for a long time afterwards the sad, haunting expression on Bertie's face.

'Difficult,' Bertie said gruffly.

Bassett thought he understood.

CHAPTER 20

Partly to avoid Helen should she be on the prowl, but mainly because an outdoor man—wellingtons—would enter his home by a back door, Bassett went to the rear of Tom Johnson's house. He knocked politely on each of the doors he found, and on the french windows; no reply, nor did any handle yield to pressure.

He progressed to greenhouse and shed, shed unlocked, greenhouse padlocked; to a paved area leading down to a lily-pond; and through a truly magnificent garden to the vegetable plot, where from habit, the curse of a good copper, even a retired one, he dabbled in speculation about the missing bag, cut up small, buried under earth or deep in the compost heap.

Sounds heard a few seconds ago registered; he sensed someone behind him, turned casually, and: 'Mr Johnson! Do forgive my cheek. I couldn't resist a tour. Your garden must be glorious in high summer!'

'Forgiven.' He was less surly today; pleasant in fact.

His hair was pale sand rather than fair, Bassett saw; and thinning. Conservatively cut. As were his clothes. He was wearing shirt and tie, corduroys not jeans, shoes not wellingtons. More the teacher than the gardener.

'We are trying to establish Shirley's frame of mind. You were tutoring her. Could we discuss that?'

'What is there to discuss?' They had walked automatically to the house. He produced a key. 'Come in.'

'Sorry if you've left your work,' Bassett said, as he followed him into a modern pine and Laura Ashley kitchen of farmhouse dimensions.

'The work will get done, my time is my own. Sit down. I'm going to have a drink. Join me?' He opened the fridge. 'Beer? Coke? Milk?' He poured milk into a glass, drank a mouthful. Milk would do nicely for him, Bassett said. 'If you can spare it.'

'Plenty.' Tom Johnson smiled. 'I used to get the Coke in for Shirley.' He handed Bassett his milk.

'Civil of you. Shirley came here for lessons?'

'I've a good library, books galore for reference. It was more convenient for her to come to me.'

'A good pupil.'

'Very.' Tom Johnson sat to one side of Bassett at the table. 'She was a naturally friendly person, easy to talk to. Although she did most of the talking.'

'About what?'

'Her dreams, ambitions. She'd spell them out, then say:

I'll never get there, will I? I'm nowhere near ruthless enough. I'd tell her to stay as she was, she'd get there, only her way would take longer.'

'I've also been hearing about strawberry jam!'

'That!' Tommy laughed softly. 'Fantastic little cook. Learnt on some farm—' He broke off, choked.

'You were in love with her,' Bassett said gently.

'Yes, but she would never have known it—' Again he broke off. 'I'm old enough to be her father, for God's sake! Besides, I'm not the marrying type. Something I could never get through to Helen.' He beat a tattoo on the table-top, jumped up.

'I've something of Shirley's. Not sure what to do with it. You can perhaps help. I'll fetch it.'

He returned with a large brown leather shoulder-bag. 'Shirley left it here last Thursday.'

'On purpose?'

'No. I walked her home after her lesson, she had her bag of books but not this one. We remembered it when we were nearly there, but she said she didn't need it. She should have collected it on Friday. She was going to come here on Friday.'

Bassett nodded slowly. 'When she didn't, you went to see where she was.'

'Yes. I bumped into Uncle Bertie; he told me she'd gone somewhere with Father Lambert. What do I do with it? Her only known relative is her mother. She is dying.'

'Have you looked inside the bag?' Bassett asked. Tom said he hadn't. 'In that case we'll do it now. Mind if I tip it out on the table?' He up-ended the bag, covered a hand with a handkerchief, and drew out the contents of two zipped compartments. 'Don't touch anything, Mr Johnson.'

'I might be lying, you think?'

'A worry only if you have a reason to lie. I'll make a list, get you to sign it.'

Collapsible umbrella, headscarf, torch, handypack of tissues, nail scissors in case, comb, hair slides, a knitting pattern, three ballpoints, notelets . . .

'She called it her Granny Bag,' Tom Johnson said with a lopsided smile. 'Everything in it.'

'Filing system, too.' The zipped compartments held Shirley's personal papers in protective bags.

Car documents; post office savings book—balance in excess of £2000; bank statements—June balance below £500; birth certificate; a receipted garage bill; another from a London garage—dated August; receipts for TV and radio sets; and a letter that had accompanied a cheque from her grandmother's solicitor.

Plus, wrapped in tissue, a ring.

'Have you seen this before, Mr Johnson?'

'I haven't seen it, no. I've heard about it.'

'From Shirley?'

No reply.

'What did you think about it?'

'It was none of my business.'

'Come on—'

'I thought Shirley had finished with the chap. She said she had.'

Bassett began refilling the bag. 'Where did you meet Shirley?' he asked conversationally.

'At Briony House, of course.'

'You hadn't met before she came to work for Mrs Pugh-Talbot?'

'No . . .' A small frown sprouted.

Bassett held his gaze for a while; believed him; slid the last item into the bag. 'I'll have to take this to the police station, Mr Johnson.' He scanned the list, looked up to see the other staring at him. Tom said nothing, however, until they were outside.

'He probably told Shirley to keep the ring.'

Bassett nodded non-committally. 'Shirley talked to you about her ambitions, her dreams. She told you she had finished with the man who gave her the ring, you say. Are you sure she never told you anything about him?'

There was a silence, then: 'He was just a man she was once engaged to. A mistake, she said.'

Bassett watched a strange sadness come over him.

'If you do think of anything, Mr Johnson—'

The man nodded dumbly, turned and jogged across the lane.

Why was love seldom simple? Bassett reflected. For Tom Johnson had loved Shirley, no doubt about it. Not much doubt that *he* knew more than he was telling either. Or Bassett was a Dutchman.

What was behind *his* reticence—guilt? Had Tom the Romantic worshipped the girl, albeit it from afar, as poets had it? And had his dream been shattered when a friend, one of those who tell you for your own good, whispered in his ear: She's not so perfect; did you know she was pregnant?

And had Tom gone to see her on Friday? Emotions all to pieces . . .

Feasible—except that *Tommy doesn't drive.*

No? Bassett pictured the man on the sit-upon mower.

And it came to him: If Tom could start an engine; if he could change gear and steer; in short, if he was able to control a motorized lawnmower, he could also have driven away the priest's car.

Erratically. Nearly running Bertie down.

The sound of a car accelerating while he was thinking these thoughts had Bassett paying rather more attention than he might otherwise have done to the car now approaching him. A glimpse of the driver was all he got, but instinctively he gave a name to the grey-haired man at the wheel. Unless he was badly mistaken he had just seen Eva Pugh-Talbot's husband, Rupert.

Driving a large BMW.

'Inspector Bob Greenaway, please.'

'Will Sergeant Miller do?'

'Do nicely . . . Andy! Is Palmer still with you?' He was. 'I've Shirley's missing bag here. She left it with Tom Johnson on Thursday. All her personal papers are in it plus bank books showing a healthy balance and nothing to suggest she was receiving money from a lover. No evidence either of her giving Palmer a handout. But—bear with me—if he was aware that she had a bit put by . . . If she was expecting him on Friday, expecting him to put the bite on . . . OK? Could explain why she left the bag at Tom's place. The ring is in the bag as well, incidentally.'

'She left the bag in Johnson's care?'

'He says not. Queer, though, for her to remember a bag of books and forget the bag *no* woman leaves behind.'

'Didn't want our friend to get his hands on it.'

'Presupposes he's a bully as well as a thief, but since his stint in gaol anything is possible. Brings me again to the burglary in July. How goes it with him?'

'Stubborn.'

'VIP's there?' Andy was pussy-footing.

'Yes.'

'Right. Tell me—did your mate recognize him?'

'He did.'

'So Palmer could not have been the pseudo-priest at seven-fifteen. He could have killed Shirley, however. For the ring. He's desperate for an injection of cash.'

'Guvnor,' Andy hissed, 'what makes you think he is strapped for cash?'

'He's driving a borrowed car. Not his style, Andy. Don't fit his image! If I were Bob I'd suggest the law might go easier on him if he confessed to killing the girl in a paddy, didn't know his own strength. Shirley's death accidental—the priest's cold-blooded, definitely. Does he want to go down for both? No mercy would be shown if he was convicted of the second murder etcetera . . .'

'Guvnor.' Still hissing. 'He knows he can't be done for the priest's murder, his alibi—'

'*Does* he know, Andy? Does he know about the priest's car driving off at seven-fifteen? *We* know. Does he?'

A second, then Andy breathed: 'What do you want?'

'The truth. Have a shot at it, see what results. I don't suppose you've had a chance to put that question? No, fair enough. Keep trying. Pen handy? Oakleigh 769. My neighbour's phone number. If I'm not at home I should be there.'

'Got it. Phone soon as I can.'

Andy did phone. Long after the sun had gone down. What he had to say stunned Bassett.

'We have another body, guvnor. By the lake. Do you know how to get here?'

'I know. Who is it?'

Andy cleared his throat. 'Uncle Bertie.'

CHAPTER 21

Emergency floodlighting beaconed Bassett to the spot. Dr Jim McPherson and the team were there; and the farmer whose stretch of water this was. Green and pleasant old England had been running short of water these past years, and John Cribbins had sworn never again to be caught out in times of drought; he had excavated, built a dam, and so provided his own water storage place. This was the 'lake'.

Huddled inside an anorak, his face drawn and grey, John was being assured that he was in no way at fault; the man doing the assuring was exceptionally tall, slim, wore a fitted sheepskin coat against an increasingly cold night temperature, and what looked to be a sheepskin hat. His voice was loud and affected, though not overbearing, his demeanour that of a successful man: Rupert Pugh-Talbot. His wife stood by, hugging a topcoat around her.

'I'm guessing no accident,' Jim McPherson said, taking Bassett to the body. 'Skull split open. I've seen damage like it done with a spade, but don't quote me yet, I need a closer look. Softish ground, see, no jagged rock to strike his head on. Have to keep an open mind for a time because he was carrying a hip flask. Barely immersed, water shallow where he was found—just there. Soles of shoes dry. He was half in, half out of the water, head first. I don't think he was in the water long.'

'I know he wasn't,' Bassett said. 'I was with him at around four o'clock this afternoon.'

Doc uncovered the dead man's face. Bassett felt cold and stiff inside. He saw Bertie at the gate, the laughing eyes, the droll 'Olé!!', and he was sorry, so very, very sorry to see the man like this.

'One over the eight? Tripped and fell?' Andy Miller had detached himself from a group of men and come to join them. 'Hit his head? On what, God knows, perimeter's been scoured once, they're going round again. Staggered this far, dizzy spell, collapsed?' He sounded angry and disbelieving.

Doc put it in a nutshell. 'Suspicious death. If you don't need me any more? PM tonight, soon as I get the body.' They thanked him, watched him go.

'Who found him, Andy?'

'The Pugh-Talbots. Apparently two of the dogs arrived without him, the other stayed at his side. No one noticed he was missing for a while. When they did they set the dogs to work, and fetched up here.'

'On foot, naturally.'

Andy followed Bassett's gaze to the large BMW on the path up from the lane. 'Hopeless,' he complained bitterly. 'Whole darned area's been trampled on; if there was some vehicle here earlier that thing has successfully obliterated any tyre marks it might have left behind.'

'Mr Pugh-Talbot's?'

'Yep. Mrs stopped here while he raced home to phone. Drove back in that.'

The farmer approached, Andy meeting him half way. An arm pointed to a light in the distance. 'That's my place if I'm wanted . . .' Simultaneously Rupert Pugh-Talbot edged towards Bassett. 'Saw you this afternoon. Bassett, isn't it? Wife's been telling me about you.' Their handshake was interrupted by a white-faced Helen Fletcher flying up the path. 'I saw the lights. The policeman wasn't going to let me through. What's going on?'

Rupert Pugh-Talbot took the initiative. 'It's Uncle Bertie, my dear. Glad you're here, I had to tell them I saw you with him this afternoon in case you had seen somebody else, somebody who could have witnessed the accident.'

'Accident?' Hysteria threatened. She craned her neck to see what the bobbing lights near the water's edge were about. 'Where is he? Is he all right?'

'He's dead, my dear.' He seemed to catch her as she fell against him. 'There, there . . .'

Bassett stole a look at Mrs Pugh-Talbot. She was in conversation with the farmer, who had delayed his departure.

Andy emerged from the darkness, Helen ran to him.

And Bassett addressed Rupert Pugh-Talbot. 'May I ask what brings you home early from London, Mr—er—?'

'Frankly, old man, you did, you and your colleagues.

This nonsense about my son. Wife can't cope. Too much. Local force troubling to visit my London office to question me, too—thought I'd best try to get to the bottom of it. Good job I am here, Uncle Bertie popping off. Wife'd be—Damn it to hell, she couldn't cope. Too much.'

'May I also ask where you were going this afternoon?'

'Wanted Helen. Told the wife she knew nothing about this boyfriend of Shirley's, but the woman must know, she saw Shirley every day. Went to her place, not there, know she does odd jobs for an elderly couple along the lane, was heading in that direction when I spotted her with Uncle Bertie on this very path, decided to see her later.'

'What were they doing?'

'Standing talking.'

'Arguing?'

'No. Far from it.'

'That would have been about half past four, shortly after you saw me,' Bassett said. 'What time was it when you noticed Uncle Bertie was missing?'

''Bout half past six. Can't say how long the dogs had been home; half an hour, thereabouts. Suddenly struck us—they were home, Uncle Bertie nowhere to be seen. Not like him to deliver them and not pop in for a snifter.' Rupert Pugh-Talbot's face caved in. 'Always drank more than was good for him. Could carry it, though. Could carry it. I never saw him legless in my life.'

Andy reappeared. Bob Greenaway next, shaking his head. Which Bassett interpreted to mean no weapon had been found; no iron bar or sharp rock on to which Bertie might have fallen.

Helen had been escorted home by a WPC.

Bassett said solicitously, 'Mrs Pugh-Talbot is looking tired.' To Bob and Mr both: 'Suppose I take her home?'

'I contacted our son, left a note for him to fetch his

mother. I'd like to stay until Uncle Bertie is taken away,' Mr said. 'But yes. If the Inspector agrees?'

Bob nodded assent. Mr went to tell her. When he was out of earshot Bassett spoke rapidly to Bob and Andy; and when Mr and Mrs rejoined them the three men appeared to be conferring. 'No option now,' Bob was saying. 'We'll have to make it public that Shirley was murdered . . .'

She sat in the passenger seat with her eyes closed, some colour slowly creeping back into her cheeks. 'Is that true? Shirley was murdered?'

'I'm afraid so,' Bassett said.

She didn't ask how. Bassett put the Citroën in gear and drove off. In darkness now he couldn't see if there was any secondary reaction. Although he sensed a kind of despair; and when he spoke to her again her replies were devoid of expression; practically lifeless.

'Your husband says it was a while before it registered that Uncle Bertie was missing.'

'Yes. The dogs were mooching in the yard. Something wrong with the dogs, Rupert said. And where is Bertie? He couldn't see Bitsa either, he's the dog that stayed behind. He went and got his hat and coat—'

'The ones he's wearing now?'

'Yes. He told me to wrap up warm, it threatened to be a cold night. I'm glad I did, it's perishing.'

They finished the short ride in silence.

Dogs and Julian poured out of the house and down the front steps to greet them.

'Only this minute got here,' Julian announced to his mother. 'How on earth did it happen?'

'Manners, Julian. Have you two met yet? This is Mr Bassett. Mr Bassett, my son.'

They shook hands. 'May I have a word while I'm here?'

Blond-haired Greek god Julian met Bassett's eyes with only a trace of anxiety. 'Yes, of course.'

His mother said, 'I trust you won't want a word with me, Mr Bassett. I should like to go to bed.'

'I'm sure tomorrow will do, Mrs Pugh-Talbot.'

She looked drained, but managed a smile. 'Thank you. Good night. Good night, Julian.'

Bassett was left standing in the hall while Julian ushered the dogs in through the house. 'I got your message from Mother,' Julian said, hastening back. 'I spoke to a Sergeant Miller. So if your query is about Friday—'

'Matter of fact, I'd like to know where you were this afternoon.'

'Oh.' Flatly. 'I was at my girlfriend's house with her mother, Aunt Barbara and others.' Uncertainty showed. 'Dad didn't say what had happened, just that Unk had been found by the lake. I thought . . . Did he fall in?'

''Afraid we won't know until the post-mortem.'

'Dead. I see. Bit of a shock.'

'I'm sorry.' The young man was swallowing rapidly. 'I should have put it more gently.'

'No other way to put it really, is there? I don't know why, but I had visions of him dripping wet and, well, he had a great sense of humour—if he'd fallen in he would simply have—have shaken himself like a dog and waved his stick at—' He tried to smile; his mouth was all wobbly. 'I'll miss him. He was a decent old—stick.'

'Might we sit down somewhere?'

'Yes, sorry. The drawing-room.' Where they remained standing, Julian as though poised for flight.

'Do you feel up to a talk about Friday?' Bassett said. 'I'm puzzled. I have it that your mother wished to discuss business with you—so told you to clear off for an hour. Seems cockeyed. She should have collared you while she had you. Would have made better sense.'

Julian grimaced. 'That's not what I said. But all right. Mother must have heard me coming, she said I needn't open the garage door, I was to disappear for a while.'

'Which you did, just like that. No argument.'

'I thought she was expecting a delivery, a surprise she didn't want me to see. My girlfriend and I—her ma and pa were coming next day to arrange our wedding among other things. Mother wanted to make an Occasion of it.'

'Perfectly reasonable. Why didn't you say that first time round?'

'It seemed childish. Surprise presents—'

'Oh, I don't know,' Bassett said amiably. 'When my wife was alive we delighted in giving each other surprise presents. You used the expression "tight-lipped" when you spoke to Sergeant Miller. Suggests displeasure. Did you mean to say it?'

'Mother wasn't expecting to see me.'

'Ah! You don't usually call in on the way to your girlfriend's home?'

'Not always. Last weekend I'd have phoned Mother from Penny's. We were going to be here on Saturday—' Julian began to lose his voice.

'You *would* have phoned your Mother,' Bassett said, not quite pouncing. 'You didn't, you came. What changed your mind?'

'I don't know. Does it matter? I can't see—'

'Did you in fact come to see Shirley?'

No reply.

'You liked Shirley.'

'I did. She was a nice girl. Penny liked her too.'

'Did you ever take Shirley out?'

'Not in the way you mean. Penny invited her to parties.'

'When was the last party?'

'April. Penny's birthday.'

'Was Shirley partnered? Attracted to anyone?'

'Did she hit it off with anybody in particular, you mean? With everybody. Penny's parents were very taken with her. And a cousin pumped me afterwards, smitten but too shy to do anything about it. I dropped a few hints to Shirley, she was flattered but nothing came of it. I let Alasdair know she was already spoken for.'

'You knew Shirley was engaged to be married?'

'Yes. She told us.'

'You believed her?'

'Whether I did or not, I managed to convince Alasdair. He didn't pine for long. He married an actress two months ago. They live in New York.'

'On Friday,' Bassett said. 'You came—and went. By which drive?'

'The back drive.'

'You'd have been able to see Shirley's door although you didn't drive past it. Did you see a car?'

'Shirley's was in the carport. I wouldn't know Father Lambert's car if I saw it, but there was another car there. Outside Shirley's door.'

'Red?'

'Blue.'

'One last question. You got here at around eight the second time. Did you stay long?'

'No.'

'What about the urgent business to be discussed?'

'Put off to another day. It wasn't that urgent when it came down to it.'

Bassett nodded. 'We'll leave it there. Thank you for your cooperation. I'm sorry about Uncle Bertie,' he added feelingly. 'I was with him this afternoon.'

'Mr Bassett—?'

'Yes?' Bassett waited.

Whatever the young man had wanted to say was left unsaid. 'I'll show you out.'

Bassett's feelings were mixed as he motored to the lake. He had found himself liking Julian Pugh-Talbot, and his instincts seldom played him false. And yet . . .

'Oh, what the heck! Everybody else appears to be hiding something, why not Julian Pugh-Talbot?'

CHAPTER 22

The scene had changed little when Bassett arrived back at the floodlit lakeside. A couple of men had turned up and announced they were from Neighbourhood Watch. Otherwise no fresh excitement.

Rupert Pugh-Talbot was reversing his BMW to a turning position; he was homeward bound.

'Where were his sympathies after we blabbed murder?' Bassett asked Andy when they met up.

'Asked was it true. Swore. Then speculated on Uncle Bertie's death: raving lunatic at large.'

Bassett's smile was grim. 'Nothing to do with them, eh? I've just seen the son. Last Friday should have been unremarkable: courtesy call on his mother, then on to his young lady's. Instead he's banished for an hour, urgency the keynote to bring him back. What happens when he gets back? The urgency no longer exists. Why? On the face of it all that happened in the interim was his mother's seeing her paying guest drive away in the company of a priest.

'The girl's condition?'

'Which Eva Pugh-Talbot says she learnt about the day before,' Bassett said.

'Therefore she was in possession of the information when she banished Julian—'

'Therefore, Andy, I am now asking myself when Eva Pugh-Talbot found out, or thought she had found out, the identity of the baby's father. Did she think *Julian*—?'

'Shirley told Helen it was Julian.'

'I think Helen lied.'

'Still, if Helen passed on the info to Eva, whose son was set to marry well—we could have a motive, guvnor. Eva was alone in the house—' he began suggestively. Then stopped. 'But by her own admission.'

'An oft-repeated admission,' Bassett said. 'Think of what she was actually doing. She was alone. By alone she means no one else around. Big house, she doing what women do when they get home from work. Much could go on without her knowing; the priest, or anyone else for that matter, could have come and gone, unheard, unseen. Pure chance that she spotted him. Mm? So why mention him?'

'Imperative to have it on record that the priest was off the premises before her husband and son got home?'

Bassett nodded. 'We're on the same wavelength, Andy. Consider this: a good way of providing yourself with an alibi is to alibi someone else. If A is with B miles from the scene of the crime, neither A nor B can be guilty. Conversely, if A *isn't* with B who *is* at the scene, A must be innocent. Could be Eva is one clever lady.'

'She wasn't alone.'

'And if she wasn't, who was with her?'

'Gives us our two people. Except—would a woman kill a priest? Even Joanna will admit women are superstitious, though they may deny it. Kill a priest—they needn't even be believers—and most women would live in superstitious fear for the rest of their lives.'

Bassett had been in difficulty himself with that one. He said after a pause, vaguely, 'Would a woman have enough power to knock a man out and dislodge two teeth?'

He then appeared to change the subject. 'Where is Freddie Palmer, Andy?'

'We had to let him go. He was with us all afternoon,

couldn't have killed Uncle Bertie. Or Father Lambert. Innocent of two out of three.' Andy shrugged.

'Nothing came of my suggestion, I take it.'

'He took the other way out, sucked up to our visiting colleagues. Coughed about the swag he went down for, much of it never recovered. You were right about that.'

'Go on,' Bassett said. 'I'm interested.'

'Apparently he worked with a partner who'd pretend to be catering staff, car park usher, whatever, depending on the venue. Prince Charming would lift the goods—and his partner would be long gone before an alarm was raised. No problem finding a buyer if you knew where to look—Palmer's partner did.'

'But something went wrong—because he's squealed.'

'Correct. You were right about Palmer probably being strapped for cash. His partner's nipped off with all the proceeds. Believed to have fled to the Antipodes.'

'He *is* short of the ready. He wanted the ring for the cash it would raise, legally. Was prepared to steal it if necessary; hence the gloves. Otherwise he was prepared to throw caution to the winds; too bad if he was seen paying a call on Friday. Shirley's death was unpremeditated—'

'If he'd killed her, he would have cleared out. Bob says.' Andy was almost apologetic.

'Why didn't he?' Bassett sounded almost happy. 'He heard talk in the pub on Saturday night. Couldn't clear out during the day, his car repairs kept him busy. Possible he went to the pub expressly to listen out for news. Had they found her? Who were they looking for? Imagine his surprise when—did his ears deceive him?—he learnt that someone else had inadvertently lifted him off the hook!'

'Guvnor?'

'Two murders, Andy, two murderers. Did you get to ask him that question?'

'Did he see anyone? Yes, he did. The back view of a man climbing a stile into the lane.'

'Into the lane? From a field.'

'Yes. Couldn't describe him, but he was wearing a yellow waistcoat or sleeveless pullover—'

Someone shouted. They turned to see Bob Greenaway hurrying towards them.

'We need to get together, Harry.' But not there, a frosty nip in the air. 'Can't do any more here tonight.'

All around them shadowy figures were packing up, some lights were being extinguished.

'Frogmen in the morning,' Bob said, breathing on cold hands. 'I'll leave a couple of men and a car here overnight. Have to see the Fletcher woman—' This to Andy. 'Then—' to Bassett—'how will you be fixed?'

It was ten p.m. 'Give me an hour, Bob. See you in the office at eleven.'

'Good.' Bob tossed his head. 'Let's steal a march on this lot.' Meanwhile the personnel carriers, revving up.

Bassett allowed himself to get lost in the exodus. When he got to Tom Johnson's house he stopped and sat in his car for several minutes before going to the house. His heart was heavy. For he had seen a yellow waistcoat hours ago, on the back of a chair in Tom's kitchen.

'Uncle Bertie is dead.'

'Yes. Helen told me. She's distraught. How did it happen?' His voice was flat and expressionless.

'Not sure, Mr Johnson.'

'Foul play?'

Bassett gave him a small smile. 'Why do you say that?'

'I'm no fool, sir.'

'Where were you this evening?'

'Here.' He finished work at five-thirty, Tom Johnson said; came home, bathed, cooked a meal. True, so far as

Bassett could judge: pots and pans in the sink, plate, knife, fork and mug on the draining-board for washing up. A meal of meat, vegetables, gravy. Not a fast meal to prepare, and cooking smells had dissipated.

'Then I wrote an order for timber. Mrs Blest wants a pergola, I'm going to build it for her.'

Builder's catalogue, drawings, ruler, pencils, and an envelope presumably containing an order form, spread on the kitchen table served to indicate, again, that the man spoke the truth. They hadn't been there earlier.

'How did you get on with Uncle Bertie?'

'I liked the old gentleman.' He spoke with warmth.

'May we talk about Shirley?'

'I thought we already had.' Flat and expressionless, but eyes over-bright like a woman's.

'Did you know she was expecting a baby?'

'Yes.'

'Yours?'

'No.'

'How long had you known?'

With each question the man had sagged a shade more. Now an eyelid began twitching. He crossed to a window, and stood looking out into blackness.

'I found out on Friday.'

'From Helen?' A calculated guess.

'Helen, yes.' He turned to face Bassett. 'She had it firmly fixed in her head that Shirley and I were—fond of each other. She was wrong, we were friends, never lovers. She was also sure in her own mind that the baby wasn't mine, she thought Shirley was making a patsy out of me. I—'

'Yes?'

'After I knocked off work I went to the flat.'

'And?'

'Shirley was in bed. Normally, a woman in bed, I'd have turned heel. I didn't. We talked. She was annoyed. About

Helen. She hadn't told Helen, Helen had witnessed a bout or two of morning sickness, and had figured it out for herself. She wouldn't tell me who the man was, she said I would be disgusted if I knew the circumstances. She also said he would never acknowledge paternity, she was going to accept full responsibility. That gave me courage.'

He continued with some emotion: 'I said she wouldn't have to face it alone, I loved her, would she marry me? I'd sell up, take her anywhere in the world she wanted to go, to start a new life. She cried.'

As he did now, silently, tears streaming down his cheeks unchecked. 'She promised to think it over. Told me she didn't love me; but I knew that. She was—sweet. Beautiful. We held hands.'

Bassett waited while he used a handkerchief. Then: 'When did you expect to see her again?'

'Later that same evening. A standing arrangement. Helen does a few hours' barmaiding on Friday evenings, it was the one night I had Shirley to myself, no Helen popping in to keep us company.' The smile reappeared. 'We were like a couple of kids doing something we shouldn't. I'd watch out for Helen going off on her bike, then I'd go to meet Shirley. All we did was cook a meal, spaghetti more often than not.'

'And last Friday should have been the same?'

With one small difference.

'Shirley was expecting a visitor, seeing him around seven o'clock, she said. She had been going to phone me to say she would be late. We agreed to meet at half past seven.'

'She was seeing him, you said. A man.'

'She said him.'

'And meet. She was going out to meet this man, and meet you afterwards.'

'I don't know. I don't think so.' A headshake. 'I had the

impression he was going to the flat. As soon as he left, she said, she would start walking.'

'What time did you leave here to meet her?'

'Quarter past. A slow stroll. She didn't come.'

'Did you go to the flat?'

'Not then. I'd have liked to know who he was, but I didn't want Shirley to think I was spying on her. In any event, I decided it would be better if I never knew who he was.'

'You thought he was the baby's father?'

'I thought it a possibility. I don't know. I just don't know. I went to the flat in the end, getting on for eight. There was no light on. I thought she had gone to bed, or was sitting in the dark, avoiding me.'

'Did you try her door?'

'No, she'd said she would think over my proposal. It was up to me to be patient. I did go for a walk round the grounds, though, in case I might spot her. That was when I bumped into Uncle Bertie.'

'Who told you she had gone with Father Lambert. Tell me—after she died, why didn't you come forward?'

'Would it have altered anything?'

'You mean you believed what was said to have happened?'

'What else? Shirley had said I would be disgusted.'

'May I recap?' Bassett said. 'How soon after five o'clock did you go to the flat?'

'As soon as I finished. I saw Shirley arrive. Mrs Pugh-Talbot was choosing flowers for her dinner-party the next day; we went round the cut-flower beds, then she came with me to the shed. I collected my jacket. It would have been about five-fifteen when I finally got away.'

'Mrs Pugh-Talbot went straight into the house?'

'Yes.'

'Did you tell her you were going to see Shirley?'

'No, I didn't.'

'So in effect she waved you off, would have assumed you were going home. How long were you with Shirley?'

'About twenty minutes.'

'You then came home. And did what?

'Glass of milk. Wash and change. Listened to some of the six o'clock news, the last ten minutes.'

'And went out again.'

'Out again?' It dawned. 'Yes. I went to get my cigarettes and lighter, I'd left them in the shed.'

'The shed in the garden at Briony House.'

'Yes.'

'Can you recall what you were wearing?'

Frowning, Tom Johnson looked down at himself. 'Much the same as now.'

Which were tan corduroys, tweed shirt, woollen tie; and a hand-knitted canary yellow waistcoat.

'I think that's all I need bother you with for now, Mr Johnson. I'll leave you in peace.'

'Come out the front way.'

The porch light lit Bassett's path after the door had shut behind him. Pinpricks of light in the distance. Some muffled motorway rumbling far off. No other sign of life. Yet he stood waiting for his night eyes, and listening . . . For as he and Tom Johnson had uttered their good nights he had been aware of movement out there in the darkness, and what had sounded like human footfalls. Not rabbit or fox.

Presently he trod silently down the path, slowing when he hit the lane. He could see now: a shadowy figure in the lane up ahead. A woman. The lamp she carried had flashed down on the hem of her skirt, betraying her. The lamp must have slipped: it and the skirt vanished, blotted out as she sped on.

He stood debating what to do, was patting a pocket for his pipe, when a light came on upstairs. He looked up:

mottled glass; the bathroom. 'Cheers, Tom,' he murmured. He reckoned on having five minutes. Made his way to the back of the house and Tom's garden shed.

The shed was unlocked, the door creaked but made no great protest as he pulled it open. He shone his pocket torch into the dark interior, bringing colour to sacks of turf dressing, bulb fibre, bone meal; to lawnmower, saws, shears, besom broom, before resting on what Bassett called 'tools'—the forks, hoes, rakes, spades. How many spades? There had been two earlier in the day. His torch found only one. He rechecked all corners. One spade only.

Chancing his arm, he sped to the kitchen garden: Tom had cooked vegetables tonight; had he left the spade in the ground? No. Nor had Bassett expected to find a spade out in the open. Tom was too careful with his tools, all the tools in the shed were speckless, as if cleaned and polished after every use.

The bathroom light went off as he reached his car.

The sounds of his driving off would be masked by plumbing noises. He hoped.

CHAPTER 23

'Who is it?'

'Harry Bassett!' He had knocked in vain three times; hadn't thought of bated-breath silence until at last Helen opened the door a crack and he saw that she was pale and shaking. 'Someone here?' he mouthed.

She mouthed No; found her voice. 'Thank heavens it's you,' she squeaked. 'Stupid me, I've never been afraid of the dark before.' All right now though, panic over. 'Come through, I was brewing a pot of tea.'

Bassett was led into a living-room that had seen better

days and better housekeeping, but was made wonderfully cosy by the glow of a wood fire. A kettle was re-plugged in and whistled instantly.

He watched Helen busy herself with tea-things. *Afraid of the dark?* She was wearing a skirt and walking shoes. An outdoor jacket hung on a peg. Torch and gloves lay on a dresser. 'Weren't you in the lane just now?'

'Oh, I wasn't scared to go out,' she said, reading him. 'It was what they said. It suddenly hit me.'

'What who said?' he inquired amiably.

'Mr Pugh-T first. Telling me how Shirley hadn't taken her own life, she'd been murdered. Is it true?' Flashing a glance.

'Did he say how?' Bassett quizzed gently.

'No. He heard the police say it. That would be why they were pestering about her boyfriend, he said. If the boyfriend had found out about her and Father Lambert—well, people had been murdered for less.'

Tea was poured. At Helen's invitation Bassett sat opposite her at the table. 'Tell me why you were frightened.'

She related it slowly in fits and starts, but the gist was there. Mr Pugh-Talbot had come straight from the lake. He'd looked quite poorly, shock upon shock. Uncle Bertie's death—plain what the police had in mind; hadn't he heard them saying Shirley was murdered? He had asked whose baby it was, why all the secrecy? Was it a secret? Or a case of everybody knowing but them, the Pugh-Talbots?

Helen had pleaded ignorance, saying Shirley had been secretive about most things. Mr Pugh-Talbot had started to lose patience. 'I'm sure I would have ended up telling him about Julian, the way he carried on, if the police hadn't shown up when they did.' Sergeant Miller and a WPC, asking about Uncle Bertie, Helen being, so far, the last person to see him alive. 'I told them he was fine when I left him.'

And on to: 'After they'd gone I couldn't stand to be on my own. It was horrible. I decided to go and ask Tommy if I could sleep on his sofa.'

She was starting up Tommy's path when the front door began opening eerily—downright spookily!—as if someone was sneaking out. 'Or hovering, waiting for me to walk into his clutches. It hit me. Somebody was going round murdering people! I ran!'

She hadn't been running when Bassett saw her; about the door, however, she was right. Tom Johnson was not a loud man, neither was he, and they hadn't been speaking at the time Tom opened the door.

Oh, vivid imagination! If Helen had held on for a few seconds she would have heard their good nights. But he could not mock her moment of terror.

She did that herself. 'I can laugh about it now.'

She repeated what she had told the Sergeant: she had gone for a bike ride after a tiff with Uncle Bertie, had cooled down, wanted to apologize, met him by the path to the lake, and spent time with him and the dogs. 'I wasn't able to stay very long, I'd promised to take Maude and Janet—' pensioner friends of her late mother—'shopping in Gleve-bourne. Late-night opening but they like to get there by six so as to have first pick of end-of-day bargains. It would be about twenty to five when I left him.'

'Where was he when you left him?'

'On the path.'

'Where you were when Mr Pugh-Talbot drove by.'

A nod. 'He was looking for me, and of course when he tried again I'd gone for Maude and Janet.'

'Did he say he'd tried again?'

'No,' Helen replied. 'But if he had—'

'He would have turned round farther on and come back?'

'He could have gone the circle, round to Sally's Lane

and home via the main drive. He must have, I think, I was in till after five, I'd have seen or heard him.'

'And he would have seen you: he would have called in here when he saw you were no longer with Bertie. Before five you would have been in.'

Helen nodded: yes. A lively yes. Followed by a tiny frown. She had both elbows on the table, both hands round her tea mug. A hand jerked so that she spilled some tea.

'There's a tree down in that field. Uncle Bertie was going to sit on it and finish smoking his cigar.'

Bassett waited for her to go on. There must be some significance to the remark. She didn't. She looked away and back again with a small sad smile. 'And sup a drop of highland oil?' Bassett said.

'Well . . .' she began indulgently. She lowered her eyes. 'I was going to say it never did him any harm.'

Fond memory, Bassett thought. He left it a moment, then: 'How do you get your ladies to their shopping? You have a car?'

'They have. I cycle to their house, leave my bike, have supper with them after the shops, bike home.'

'Where do they live?'

'The old manor house on the main road.'

She wouldn't have passed the lake.

'You didn't see the activity when you were returning from your ladies,' Bassett accused, not unkindly.

'No,' Helen said sheepishly. 'Bill Storey told me. He went past in his van, was turning out on the main road as I was cycling in. He pulled up to ask me if I knew what was going on.'

The next second Bassett found himself being stared at in a most discomforting manner. 'It was your car outside Tom Johnson's!' Helen said ferociously.

He blinked. Hadn't she recognized it earlier? No, possibly not in the dark.

'You're picking on Tommy! All of you! I see it all now. Why Mr P-T came to dig at me, why Mrs has been pumping me unmercifully. Julian's peccadillo is out! But darling Julian mustn't have his name besmirched, oh no, let Tommy be the scapegoat, let Tommy take the blame! But he didn't do anything to Shirley, I should know, I was there, I saw Tommy leave! I—'

The tirade ceased abruptly. 'What have I *said*?' she whined. 'Tommy didn't do it,' she said, running down.

'I know Tommy was there, Helen. He told me himself.'

'I don't believe you.'

'I'm not in the habit of telling lies.'

She eyed him. 'No. Sorry.'

'Why not tell me your side of it.'

'I saw Tommy leave Shirley's flat. She was perfectly all right, I heard her talking to Mrs Pugh-Talbot, she was still talking to her when Father Lambert arrived.'

'Just a second,' Bassett said amiably. 'You weren't at the house when Shirley got home from the Graylings'.'

'My afternoon off. I went to see Shirley. To see if Tommy had said anything to her.'

'About the baby. You told him about the baby.'

'I did. She was doing the dirty on him. I know they pretended to be just friends, but I also saw how he would look at her when he thought no one was watching. He was dotty about her. She didn't deserve him.'

'Are you saying Tommy was the boyfriend? If so, you fibbed. You told me you didn't know who he was.'

'I said Shirley never *told* me. They were clever at hiding it. Even to writing letters to her imaginary man. Normal post she would leave in the kitchen for the postie to collect with the house mail, but once a week this one particular letter she insisted on posting herself. To him, she said, the boyfriend. Supposed to be abroad, but no one ever saw an airmail sticker. And, as I think I told you, there was never a letter from him to her.'

'You are fond of Tommy,' Bassett said gently. 'You had hopes of you and he—?'

'I had to tell him. It seemed the right thing to do. Yes, I am fond of him, that's why I did it. For what good it did,' she said sorrowfully. 'He was all over her, soft and protective. He didn't hurt her, he worshipped her.'

'You said you heard them—'

'Yes. I started up the stairs to the flat, and they were talking. Tommy was gentling her, saying he loved her, would she marry him, he'd be so proud, the child would be theirs, his and hers. I couldn't bear to listen, so I went and stood in the tackle shed. There's a hole in the wall, I could see when he left. Then I tried again. Tommy would never have told me the outcome, Shirley might.'

'Even though you blackened her to Tommy?'

'He wouldn't have told her it was me, he's too nice. I never got the chance anyway, Mrs Pugh-Talbot was there. Shirley must have been in bed, Mrs Pugh-T was asking if she'd like a cup of tea.'

'This would have been about half past five?'

'About that.'

'Why did you choose that particular time to go?'

'It was either then or after I'd finished at the Pig and Whistle. I do some bar work on Fridays.'

'Didn't give Tommy much time. Shirley had been at the Graylings' all day.'

'I know. Oh, it's not true, what I just said.' She waved it away. 'Have you ever done something you regretted as soon as you'd done it? What I was really hoping to do was get there before Tommy, I thought he'd probably wait anyway until she went for her lesson. I was going to own up, tell he what I'd done.'

'That is more believable,' Bassett said, smiling. 'What did you do when you heard Mrs Pugh-Talbot?'

'Waited at the bottom of the stairs for her to go.'

'Hear what was being said?'

'Some of it. It was the baby's father Mrs Pugh-T was interested in, trying to drag the name out of Shirley. Was it Julian, Bertie, Mr Pugh-Talbot, Julian again. I think she must have pulled the door to after that. They carried on talking but I couldn't hear properly. I got fed up and went outside for a smoke. Not long after that I heard a car coming so I cleared off.'

A *car*. 'Whose car, Helen?'

'Father Lambert's, I suppose. Although at the time I thought of the doctor. If Shirley was ill she could have sent for him.'

'You didn't stay to see?'

'I couldn't hang about indefinitely, I had my other job to go to.'

'What time did you get home?'

'A quarter past six, twenty past. I had to rush to get washed and ready, I know that.'

'You came straight here? Takes five minutes?'

'Yes.' No, she had to collect her bike from the old tackle room. 'Say ten.'

'So you heard the car at ten past six at the latest?'

'Yes . . .' She began to look puzzled.

Father Lambert was still at the presbytery then.

'Why do you want to know these times?' She seemed vaguely amused.

'Bear with me,' he said in like vein. 'You heard a car, didn't see it. Didn't peep through the hole?'

Too miserable to bother, Helen said; and thinking of Shirley. 'She told Mrs Pugh-T she had everything under control. Poor Shirley, she didn't know Father Lambert was about to turn up. She wasn't expecting *him*.'

'How do you know this?' Bassett said quietly.

'I took his call, didn't I? When I went for a smoke. I went to the kitchen for a match. The phone rang. It was Father Lambert. He wanted to speak to Shirley, but Shirley wasn't answering. She'd probably pulled the plug; she did sometimes, when she wanted to be left in peace to study and so on. Anyway, she was in, I told him. He said excellent, he was on his way. So you see—Tommy couldn't have hurt Shirley, could he? He'd long gone.'

She started to cry, softly.

Bassett watched her. 'Would you like to go to an hotel tonight, Helen? Friends of mine. Be waited on for a change, breakfast in your room. I could pick you up in the morning in time for work.'

'Be a lady for a night?' Her eyes shone. 'Luxury.' With her face blotchy and damp from crying she was almost childlike. But no. She shook her head. 'It's kind of you, but I'd rather stay here. I feel better now we've had this talk. You've done me good.'

'If you are sure.'

'I am, thank you.' They smiled at each other.

'May I ask one last question? On Friday, did you see anybody else? A stranger in the area?'

'I didn't see a thing. I was so *miserable* I couldn't concentrate on anything. I wish I could tell you I saw a stranger, but I didn't. I'm sorry.'

Bassett didn't remind her to bolt the door after he went, he'd no wish to bring hobgoblins back; but he waited until he heard the bolt slide into place before leaving altogether.

This time he glanced in as he passed the living-room window: Helen was standing in front of a mirror messing with her hair, piling it on top of her head, preening, shaking the hair free; and now moving towards the pantry door.

'Practising coquetry?' Bassett murmured, as he walked on. For whose benefit? he wondered.

In his car he reflected on her delight when he had suggested a night at an hotel. He was sure she had been on the verge of accepting. What had prompted the refusal? An assignation she had temporarily forgotten about?

He drove towards Briony House, parked beyond the entry to the tradesmen's drive, walked back.

Nearly there he spotted the shaft of light, her front door opening . . . her shape. She was carrying something. He tucked himself well into a high hedge, holding his hat over the lower part of his face lest she shine her lamp in his direction . . . She did not. But she did flick it on once after reaching the lane; to get her bearings.

Helped him too. *She was carrying a spade.*

He followed. Tom Johnson's house was in darkness save for chinks of light from a bedroom window. Helen's lamp flashed on as she crept along the side of the house to the rear. She returned without the spade.

Some minutes later Bassett paid another visit to Tom Johnson's shed. Two spades, both polished as new.

Oh! Helen, he sighed. How you must love your Tommy!

CHAPTER 24

A flask of hot soup and sandwiches awaited Bassett in Bob Greenaway's office, compliments of Andy's Joanna.

On Bob's desk were the contents of Bertie's pockets. The cheroot case contained two cheroots, as it should have done, there being three in the case when Bertie proffered them. Bassett had declined, Bertie took one out to smoke. 'Found this by the lake,' Andy said. He held up a plastic envelope which contained a butt.

All three of them gazed at the butt as if willing it to tell them something. It did not.

'We've been kicking it around, Harry.' Bob meant facts, speculation, not the butt. 'Rupert Pugh-Talbot. No alibi for last Friday. Only his word for it that he got home after the priest's car drove off. Comes home a day early this week—and we have another death.'

Motive? 'He's a Lloyd's underwriter, recently lost a packet. He has financial problems, and you know how some of these families work: Julian admits to paternity—his girl's dad isn't going to lift a finger to help *his* dad, is he?'

Would he anyway?

'Maybe not with cash, but *contacts*. If you want to stay at the top you cultivate those at the top, you do not alienate them. What if Mrs Pugh-T, knowing about Shirley's condition and the son's possible involvement, passed the info on to her husband? He hotfoots it home, say to buy the girl off. Mrs watches out for Julian, despatches him. Then, what if Shirley won't be bought?'

Mr coming home before eight o'clock could fit, Bassett told them. He gave them a brief run-down of his meetings with Tom Johnson and Helen. When he got to what Helen had said about the car—'Whose car? I asked. Reply: Father Lambert's, I suppose, although at the time I thought it was the doctor's.

'She thought doctor because she'd heard Mrs Pugh-T remark on Shirley being in bed—illness. Subconsciously she knew it couldn't be Father Lambert because she was the one who took that call. He told her he was on his way—and he couldn't have got there in the time. We know it wasn't a doctor. Or Father Lambert. Or Palmer.'

All three exchanged glances. Rupert Pugh-Talbot?

Mr and Mrs? In it together? Bob Greenaway was all for it, until Andy pointed out: 'Mrs is a Catholic.'

'Meaning she wouldn't be a party to murdering a man of the cloth?' Bob scoffed. 'Maybe not before the event. But presented with a fait accompli—the girl dead, priest out cold—loyalty to her marriage if not her husband would be an overriding factor. She'd help him rearrange the evidence.'

Or, since they were only kicking it around—*he* came to *her* assistance. She might have throttled Shirley while trying to shake the truth out of the girl.

Take the spade. Was it common knowledge that Tom's shed wasn't locked? If so, anybody could have taken a spade. Rupert Pugh-Talbot, for one. Helen wouldn't see him go past before she went to collect her pensioner ladies—he didn't get that far. He only got as far as Tom Johnson's.

But if Rupert Pugh-T took the spade why did Helen do the replacing? Something going on between them, perhaps?

Bassett shook his head, not really a negative gesture. 'One possibility. To protect Tom. Suppose when he went to dig up vegetables tonight for his tea he discovered he was a spade short. She called in to tell him about Bertie, an accident which common sense would suggest wasn't an accident. And suppose Tom told her about his missing spade?'

'Why not tell us?' Bob said.

'He, because he didn't want to be in any deeper than he already is. She, because she's half convinced we are bent on making a scapegoat of Tommy.'

'She take her own spade, guvnor?'

'I didn't stop to check, Andy. Tom seemed to have gone to bed. The spade should be safe till morning.'

'I'll have the house watched anyway.' Bob made a note.

Kick it around from another angle. What about Helen and Tom Johnson? That business with the cub reporter: was Helen's blabbing really done in all innocence?

Bassett said he thought not.

'Mischief-making?' Andy said.

'Helen a stirrer, a wooden-spoon merchant?' Bassett

shook his head. 'I thought so once, I'm better informed now. I think she deliberately linked Shirley and the priest in order to protect Tom Johnson. From what? Murder charges? Not then, no. Try this: she heard Tom Johnson declare his love for Shirley; he was all soft and protective, she said. And the very next day—there Shirley was, with the priest, both dead. What an idiot Tom would feel! A prize idiot! She was protecting him from being made to look a fool.'

He found himself being stared at again. He shrugged. 'She is crackers about the man.'

'Why did she tell the lot tonight?' Bob said.

'Change of circumstances. Murder has been uttered. *Now* she is protecting him from murder charges. He didn't do it, didn't kill Shirley, he couldn't have, Shirley was still alive when he left her, she knew.'

'Alibied.'

'Both of them,' said Andy.

'Up to six o'clock,' Bassett said.

What about the chap wearing a yellow waistcoat?

'Tom Johnson,' Bassett said. 'After leaving Shirley he washed, changed, realized he'd left his cigarettes in the big house garden shed, and went back for them.'

Bob Greenaway picked that up. 'Helen knew the priest was coming. Suppose, stirring some more, she ran to tell Tommy after she left her listening post . . . Then, today—what if Uncle Bertie said something that alarmed her, and again she rushed to cant to Tommy—'

Bob liked his own idea, as far as it went. Andy was watching Bassett. Bassett had stopped listening, he was seeing a series of images flashing on a screen inside his head . . . here, fuzzy . . . there, superimposed by unrelated images . . . Seemingly unrelated. Maybe not . . .

'Harry? Any comment?'

'What? Whatever you say. We're kicking it around, aren't we?'

There they left it. Bassett had been going to say a piece about Freddie Palmer. But Andy and Bob hadn't thought to mention him, so neither did he.

The night wasn't over for Bassett. One a.m. Starry sky. Telephone ringing as he entered the house.

'Bassett.'

'Julian Pugh-Talbot here. You know Jack Carter, he writes country books—'

'As Jack the Poacher, yes.'

'My girlfriend Penny knows his wife, Helen. Pen was telling Helen about Shirley and—look, I'm not making a very good job of this. Helen suggested we talk to you, we could rely on your discretion. Pen and I would like to see you now, tonight. I know it's late, but—'

'Do you know how to find me?'

'We already did, we were sitting outside your cottage for an hour.' A pause, muffled sounds, a hand covering the mouthpiece: 'He'll see us, Pen.' Strongly, to Bassett: 'We can be there in fifteen minutes, probably less.'

Bassett took to Julian's girlfriend on sight. It was her big violet eyes that smiled bewitchingly when he opened the door to them, her mouth that framed the introduction: 'Jules and Penny.' She who chattered nervously as he hung up their coats, first apologizing for the scarlet mohair sweater now revealed: 'Far too bright—not disrespectful—I couldn't find anything warm yet duller in a hurry—so *cold* all of a sudden,' and then apologizing for the lateness of their call. It was she also, when they were settled in front of the gas fire, her presence giving the room almost a festive air, their hands wrapped round steaming mugs of hot chocolate, who exclaimed, 'This is fun, I haven't had cocoa for ages!'—and then soberly referred to what had brought them.

'We couldn't see anything to be gained by coming before, but now Julian's dad has told us Shirley was murdered there are things you ought to know. But I'll let Julian tell you, I'm hopeless, truly, I rabbit. I'm a terror, aren't I?' To Julian.

He grinned. 'A monster.'

He turned to Bassett. 'It's good of you to see us.'

'One thing,' Bassett said. 'I promise confidentiality unless I consider it necessary to pass on what you tell me. The promise extends to letting you know beforehand if I do. Do I make myself clear?'

They exchanged looks and nodded. 'We agree.'

'I didn't tell the whole truth before,' Julian said. 'I did go home to see Shirley last Friday. Mother did meet me, as I said. I didn't argue because I thought I knew why she was cross. I thought she'd found out about the abortion.'

Bassett moved not a muscle.

'When she told me to disappear for an hour I thought she wanted time with Shirley herself. Mother is a Catholic, you see. Dad isn't, I'm not. I was sure Shirley wouldn't have said anything to her, but someone else might have done. Anyhow, that was why I cleared off as bidden, and why I came back later. I was prepared for a row, but I'd face it and nip in and have a word with Shirley while they were having their meal. I tried to phone Shirley from the Black Swan, but got no reply. I didn't know, of course, that she had gone off with Father Lambert.'

'May I ask when you learnt that?'

'The next day, or Sunday. I can't remember.'

'It wasn't when you returned at eight o'clock?'

'No. When I got back—nothing. I was puzzled, but I thought Shirley would tell me what had happened. I went to her flat, it was in darkness but the door was unlocked,

I thought she had left it unlocked for me. She wasn't there. I looked for a note from her. There wasn't one, so I went straight on to Penny's, thinking Shirley would phone us if she still wanted to go ahead.'

'Go ahead with the abortion?'

'Yes.'

'Tell me about it,' Bassett said.

Julian glanced at Penny. She said, 'Shirley came to one of my parties. She never seemed to go anywhere, and we liked her, she'd been wonderful with Julian's grandmother, and, well, I invited her. Well, some of my friends are open and matter-of-fact about sex and living together, that kind of thing,' she said awkwardly. 'They don't flaunt it, their views I mean, but I rather think Shirley overheard certain things that were said, because about four weeks ago she rang me, said she had to have an abortion, and we—Julian and I—were the only ones she could turn to. She referred to our friends, a certain clinic and so on, and begged the address . . . You carry on, Julian.'

Julian cleared his throat. 'She couldn't report the rape, she said, no one would believe her. She'd been engaged to the man, had written to him for nearly two years when he was in prison, he was released in July and only a dimwit would believe she hadn't slept with him of her own free will.

'We gave her a telephone number. Nothing backstreet, Mr Bassett. The clinic has Ministry of Health approval. Everything was to be done legally.

'Then a fortnight ago she phoned us again. She had been accepted some time ago to start nursing training in January, but the hospital had contacted her to offer her a place at the end of September. She wanted to take up the offer. Her date for the clinic was Tuesday, the Tuesday just gone. On balance she felt it best to leave Glevebourne altogether when she went to the clinic, rest up for several days, and move straight to her nursing digs. She'd recalled one of Pen's friends saying her home was available for the odd weekend in London. Would this friend take her as a paying guest for a fortnight? We fixed it up for her.'

Penny: 'Julian would have felt disloyal for helping her to do a moonlight flit if she'd still worked for his mother, but as matters stood the fewer who knew her plans the better. Our friends were going to collect her while we were at the dinner-party on Saturday.'

'That's why I was going to see Shirley on Friday,' Julian said. 'To finalize arrangements.'

Penny shrugged theatrically. 'Is all.'

'But your mother intervened,' Bassett said, addressing Julian. 'You didn't tell her you had an appointment with Shirley?'

A headshake. 'I made the excuse that I wanted to hose my car down before going on to Penny's.'

'To which your mother replied?'

'That I could leave the garage doors alone, and—'

'Ah,' Bassett cut in. 'The hose lives in the garage, I take it. Whose doors were shut.'

'Yes . . .'

That out of the way, Bassett contemplated the two young people, said kindly, forestalling their obviously growing curiosity, 'I'm guessing that something happened to what you rushed here to say earlier; you had to wait so long *impact* has been lost. I mean of course—the rape. You've barely touched on it.'

Oh, those beautiful eyes of Penny's! So expressive.

'Do either of you know Freddie Palmer?'

Julian nodded. 'I've met him. Before he went down. I'd no idea he and Shirley . . . Until she told us.'

'If you had known?'

'I should have warned her off.'

'Persona non grata,' said Penny.

'Which may account for him not wishing to show himself at your parents' home, Julian. Especially after the July burglary?' Bassett made this a question.

'He did it, Mr Bassett. It was also his baby. When Shirley learnt about the burglary she was sure he did what he did to her in order to shut her up; she couldn't very well shop him for the burglary without incriminating herself. She couldn't tell anybody but us. Others would have preached, counselled, pitied. She didn't need that. Worse, she didn't want her child to be as unhappy as she had been. You know she spent most of her life in foster homes?'

'A *love*-child can be happy,' Penny said emotionally. 'But nobody wants to know they exist solely as a result of an attack on their mother. That's why we helped Shirley.'

'I understand,' Bassett assured her. 'Tell me—I'm baffled. If Shirley couldn't bring herself to confide all to Father Lambert, and she had a private clinic booked, why did she visit her own doctor and her priest last week, do you know?'

'We think she was wavering,' Penny said. 'And went to the doctor's as if, well, as if the clinic had never existed. She was starting from scratch.'

Julian agreed. 'It wouldn't have surprised us if she'd cancelled the clinic at the last moment. She hated the idea.

'As for Father Lambert—she went on Tuesday to tell him she was leaving Glevebourne. She hadn't intended telling him why, but he got it out of her, then demanded to know the name of the man responsible for her condition. She wouldn't tell him a name or *how*, he would have got straight on to the police, which was the last thing she wanted. He asked her to think it over, and go and see him again on Friday.

'In the interim she realized she might have worried him unnecessarily. She hadn't given him the London address, she had simply said she had a place to go to; but she knew it had come out badly, as if she were fobbing him off, and he probably had visions of her ending up homeless or something equally unpleasant—'

'She phoned me about it,' said Penny. 'She had also been vague about *when* she was leaving. I said it wouldn't hurt to give him our friend's address, it was a private house, not the clinic. She could use it to put his mind at rest—tell him she'd got fixed up definitely, and would be moving out over the weekend. She said she would do that.'

Julian again: 'I don't know why Father Lambert would have gone to see her later. Unless it was to make another attempt at getting a name out of her. He had tried again in the morning.'

'You spoke to her after she saw him in the morning?'

'She phoned me from the Graylings', yes. She gave him the address, told him she was leaving. Nothing more.' He turned to Penny. 'The letter, Pen—'

Penny opened her shoulder-bag; handed Bassett a white unsealed envelope addressed to Father Lambert.

Julian explained: 'When I was looking for a note from Shirley I found that. I took it because Shirley had told me she was writing a letter to Father Lambert which she wanted Penny and me to hold on to until, well, she would let us know when to post it. She said she had to write it before the event, she wasn't sure she'd be able to afterwards.'

Putting on his reading glasses, Bassett read the letter in silence. 'A case of *if* she ever wanted it posted, yes?' He refolded the letter. 'We were discussing Freddie Palmer. How would he have felt about the baby, do you think?'

'He was never to be told,' Julian said with intensity. 'That wouldn't have been the reason . . .' He faltered. 'If it was murder,' he continued hesitantly, 'there was a ring. Shirley wasn't going to give it back until she was good and ready. We think she may have been holding on to it as a form of insurance. Should she have decided to cancel everything, I mean the clinic, the ring would have financed her and the baby for quite a while.'

'That's what we think,' Penny said, round-eyed. 'Oh! it's awful! But who on earth would have wanted to murder poor Shirley except him, Freddie Palmer, the swine!'

CHAPTER 25

Friday morning. An early frost now glistening moisture on field and verges. The lakeside busy.

'Thought we had it,' Bob Greenaway said, pointing to the metal end of a spade, ancient, corroded. 'According to the experts here—' the frogmen—'this has been in the water for months. Probably buried in the field for years before that. The farmer's JCB uncovered it.'

'Museum piece,' someone commented.

Nevertheless, it was bagged. The frogmen had finished their search: new lake, clean bottom, the job had been an easy one. No sign of the real murder weapon, alas.

'Hope the Chief's in a good mood,' Bob said morosely to Bassett. 'The cost of this lot! Might cheer him up if one of Tom Johnson's spades turns out to be it, of course. We've got both, he very kindly agreed to us borrowing them.'

Bassett said nothing. What was there to say?

Bob was now returning to the station for a confab in readiness for a session for the Pugh-Talbots. 'Glad you're here, Harry, saves a phone call. Ten-thirty. At Briony House. We'll test reactions if nothing else.'

'Already had one, Bob. Julian and his girl came to see me last night. Dad told them he'd overheard Murder.'

Bob looked the question.

'They fingered Palmer,' Bassett told him.

'They would,' was Bob's sour response. 'Anything to keep it out of the family. You coming with us?'

'See you later. Errands to attend to first.'

Loose ends in fact; call them petty irritations, to clear up. Images that had popped on to that screen inside his head; had come and gone leaving question-marks behind.

Helen Fletcher's claim that she had been cycling to the post office at two p.m. on Saturday, for instance. His, Oakleigh's, village post office had been renamed Community Post Office. A misnomer in his view, since opening hours had been reduced to mornings only. How this benefited the community he had still to work out. However . . .

Helen's post office turned out to be also a shop, open all day, every day, and called by many older parishioners traditionally, 'the post office'. No lie there.

Next, the office of the *Glevebourne Gazette*, catching the cub reporter doing a solitary jig and reddening to the roots of his sandy locks when he belatedly noticed Bassett toe-tapping to the din bellowing from a portable radio. A few questions, a few eager-beaver answers, and Bassett had a clearer picture of what happened on Saturday afternoon.

One more call to make. 'Does the Pig and Whistle serve coffee?' he asked the lad.

A buzz of excitement met him when he entered Bob's office. 'We've got him!' Bob announced. 'He lied. He was here in Glevebourne at twenty to six last Friday. Filled up with petrol at Sutton's Garage. No doubt about the date or the time, he has an account there.'

'Who?' Bassett inquired, being cussed.

'Rupert Pugh-Talbot. We do have a case against him, guvnor,' Andy said, with some regret in his voice.

Bassett gestured: So be it.

Bob Greenaway paid no heed to either of them. He had cracked it, it was all his case now. 'Preliminary post-mortem results: no water in Bertie's lungs; insufficient alcohol in his system to prove inebriation; no evidence of stroke or heart attack as *cause* of death; no ankle sprain—'

In short, nothing to give weight to claim that the old man fell and struck his head. In layman's language, death was caused by injuries to the brain inflicted by a semi-sharp object, possibly, and in Doc's opinion, a spade. Rupert Pugh-Talbot had opportunity, means—notably access to a spade, possibly Tom Johnson's, and he had motive. Not only for Bertie's murder but for the other two as well.

All of this being said in a rush: an over-abundance of nervous energy, was Bassett's tranquil thought. No wonder Bob had no flesh on his bones.

Still talking: 'Chief's given us the go-ahead. A warrant is being processed. What about it, Harry?'

'You're the boss, Robert,' Bassett said.

Coffee and biscuits had been taken into the library for them. 'Compliments of Mrs Pugh-Talbot,' Helen said. 'I am to advise you that we are all in the drawing-room.'

She added, off her own bat and less pompously, 'He wants us all interviewed together.'

'Is that what you all want?' Andy asked.

'I don't think Julian is keen. Neither am I, I'll be tongue-tied in front of Mrs Pugh-Talbot. But the master has spoken,' she mumbled under her breath, departing.

Bob Greenaway bristled. '*We* call the tune. This is a murder inquiry. Go fetch Julian, Andy.'

Julian was already there, not in response to a summons, he brought a message. 'Telephone, Inspector Greenaway.'

It was the station; Bob was wanted urgently. He told Bassett: 'New evidence.'

And so it was Bassett, alone, who entered the drawing-room. He smiled at the gathering. 'Inspector Greenaway extends his apologies, he's been called away. Perhaps we could have a chat while we are waiting.'

Mrs Pugh-Talbot wasn't pleased. 'I do have business to go to. This is most inconsiderate of him.'

'Then may I beg a few minutes of your time first?' Bassett said, glancing dismissively at the others.

Rupert Pugh-Talbot elected to remain with his wife.

CHAPTER 26

'Among the first notes I made on the case,' Bassett began, 'were a series of times. At five p.m. last Friday Shirley returned from a day spent with the Grayling twins. Half an hour later you, Mrs Pugh-Talbot, went to see Shirley in her flat. At six-thirty you heard sounds that led you to think Shirley was getting ready to go out. Then at seven-fifteen, give or take, you and Uncle Bertie saw her and Father Lambert leaving together. All of which appeared to tie in with subsequent events.

'I have since added other significant times. At five-fifteen, for example, Mr Johnson went to the flat. Helen Fletcher went later. And at seven p.m. Julian arrived home on a flying visit.

'Mr Johnson says he spent twenty minutes with Shirley. Helen says she saw him leave. Afterwards she started up the stairs and heard you, Mrs Pugh-Talbot, asking Shirley if she would like a cup of tea. Which bears out what you told us, that Shirley was in bed with a headache. Helen retreated downstairs, but didn't leave.

'Why did Mr Johnson go to Shirley? He was not the mystery boyfriend or the father of the unborn child. In fact he only learnt about the baby that day. He went out of love for Shirley all the same, to offer her marriage.'

Rupert Pugh-Talbot said: 'Does he know you're telling us this? His private life—'

Bassett cut him short. 'You know already.' He turned to Mrs Pugh-Talbot. 'You have said that Shirley confided her condition to you on Thursday, the day before her death. Not true, is it? I believe the first you heard of it was when you overheard her and Mr Johnson together. You did go to the flat—but not at five-thirty, you went earlier. They didn't hear you open the access door. You listened. You then saw Mr Johnson leaving—'

'That's nonsense. If I had known Tommy had been in the flat don't you think I would have informed the police? He could have been her murderer.'

'But you didn't know she had been murdered, did you? You didn't know for certain until last night.' The slight emphasis on 'certain' was no accident. 'Nor did you know about the baby until you heard Tom and Shirley talking. Isn't that so?'

'A day's difference, Mr Bassett. Does it matter?'

'It matters that because of what you overheard you later suggested Tom for the role of elusive boyfriend.'

'I'm not proud of my behaviour,' she said softly.

'No, I'm sure eavesdropping did not come naturally. I imagine that you were initially held spellbound . . . You also heard Shirley say she was expecting someone at seven o'clock. Her refusal to name him—she told Tom he would be disgusted if he knew the full story—had you fearing the worst. That was how you came to be in the yard when your son drove in. You were waiting for Julian.'

'For anyone who might turn up, Mr Bassett.'

'But you did think Julian. Why?'

'The expression on Shirley's face when I mentioned his name. She was a—poor liar.'

'So, forgive me. I'm confused. You half expected to see

Julian, yet when he came you sent him packing. Why didn't you have it out with him there and then?'

'I wanted to speak to Shirley first.'

'To get her to drop charges, so to speak?'

'If that was what she had in mind, yes. I didn't *want* to believe it of Julian, but if he *had* been irresponsible, better he remain in ignorance of the consequences. A few words from Shirley, and his life could have been shattered. He was going to be staying at Westonby Park that weekend; even if he failed to keep his appointment with Shirley she could have got to him by telephone. Friday evening was my only opportunity to have it out with her.'

'But Helen heard you talking to Shirley long before six o'clock. You had a whole hour until seven.'

'No, I hadn't. Father Lambert came.'

'So he did. But how did you know? You have said you didn't see him arrive.' He let it go. 'You say you wanted a heart-to-heart with Shirley. Presumably you would then have tackled your son.'

'If necessary. Had I been successful Julian could, as I have said, remain in ignorance.'

'Which in fact he did. When he returned at eight p.m. you had nothing to say to him on the matter.'

'Because Shirley had gone with Father Lambert. I had begun to think I had jumped to the wrong conclusion.'

'Yes, I think I understand.' Bassett shifted his gaze to her husband, who met the gaze unflinchingly. 'I've had—been harbouring—the quaintest notion, devilishly difficult to get rid of, that when you despatched Julian your aim was to keep him from opening the garages.'

'Look here!' Rupert Pugh-Talbot was getting heated. 'I've been tolerant up to now, but damn it, man, what has this to do with Uncle Bertie's death?'

'If I might explain further,' Bassett said, appearing to give way. 'Helen overheard your wife with Shirley, she wanted to see Shirley herself, and so waited. Until—at around six o'clock she heard a car arriving, envisaged yet another visitor for Shirley, and so took herself off.

'She fancied the car was a doctor's, Shirley being in bed, ill. We know it wasn't. We also know it wasn't Father Lambert's. It was your car, Mr Pugh-Talbot, was it not?'

The man stared, threw back his head, and gave a short, sharp laugh. The kind that says: So *that*'s what this is about! 'It was.' He glanced at his wife, said to Bassett: 'What is it you want to know?'

'Why you said you got home at eight o'clock.'

'Wouldn't have if I had foreseen events. Damn silly thing to do. But if you cast your mind back, the news of the tragedy was brought to us on Saturday afternoon while our guests were here. No crime was mentioned, the police were simply attempting to establish Shirley's last movements. Uncle Bertie said he saw the couple leave, my wife verified it. Was I a third witness? I replied that I was motoring home from London at the time, got here at eight p.m. That said, I was free to return to our guests. Why prolong it? Simpler to keep it simple, if you see what I mean.'

Eva Pugh-Talbot came to his defence. 'It was as my husband says. In retrospect I realize we were incredibly selfish, thinking only of ourselves, but I don't think the news had sunk in properly.'

Bassett nodded. 'May I ask why you came home earlier than usual last Friday, Mr Pugh-Talbot?'

'Pressures of work. I'd had my fill.'

'Mrs Pugh-Talbot, I have to ask this. Did your husband influence you in supporting his lie?'

'Not at all. As he explained later—the police might have gone on to inquire how he had spent the two hours from six till eight, and he couldn't have told the truth without bringing Julian into it.'

'What was the truth, Mrs Pugh-Talbot?'

Her husband answered for her. 'That I spoke to the girl after Eva did . . . Carry on, old girl, clear the slate.'

'I was in the kitchen,' she said, 'having just come down from the flat, when Rupert came in. After we'd said our hellos I told Rupert about Shirley. Oh lordy, he said; what did Julian have to say for himself? I said I didn't think Julian knew yet—'

'So I nipped up to have a word with Shirley. Spent no more than five minutes with her. She ticked me off, said I was invading her privacy. So that was that. I bowed to her wishes. Thought I'd give her half an hour and try again.'

'You returned to the kitchen?'

'Not immediately. I changed out of my suit while I was upstairs.'

'Which took you how long?'

'I was back with Eva at twenty past six. Eva commented on how quick I had been. We both looked at Jemima.'

Jemima was the grandmother clock in the kitchen.

'What did you do then?'

'Drank a coffee, and went to put my car away. I hadn't garaged it because I thought Eva might fancy a meal out. She didn't. She'd already put something in the oven, anyway. I was in the yard when the priest arrived.'

'*You* saw the priest arrive?'

'Saw him enter the flat, yes. I told Eva I might as well do something useful while I was waiting for him to go. We'd had coloured lights installed in the garden for next day's dinner-party. Eva switched them on, I went to check that they were all working.'

'Meanwhile you, Mrs Pugh-Talbot, went upstairs, tried the access door and found it locked—which Shirley might have done herself, for privacy. This was at six-thirty.'

'Bit later,' her husband said. 'It was getting on for twenty to seven when I saw the priest. I remember looking at my watch and thinking Eva could have got it wrong, it was the priest Shirley was expecting, he'd come early.'

Bassett made mental notes: Six-twenty to six-forty, the way was clear for Shirley's murderer. If he'd arrived before Father Lambert, and left while Mr was checking the fairy lights . . .

'Did you see anyone while you were testing the lights, Mr Pugh-Talbot?'

'Only Tom Johnson. He went to the shed.'

'You spoke to him?'

'Don't think he saw me. He didn't linger anyway. In by the side gate, out the same way.'

'Did you see where he went to from there?'

'No. I didn't pay that much attention.'

'Mrs Pugh-Talbot, no offence intended, but now we know that your husband told you of Father Lambert's arrival I imagine you tried the access door the second time hoping to eavesdrop again. Were you tempted, when you found the door bolted, to go out and round to the foot of the stairs?'

'I was tempted, yes. I didn't because I wanted to listen out for Julian—'

'And prevent him from opening the garage door. Why?'

The lady sighed. 'He would have seen Rupert's car. I didn't want him to know his father was home.'

'Why not?' Still probing for something sinister.

But the answer, said without hesitation, made, as Bassett was fond of saying, perfect sense. Not necessarily pleasant sense, but sense nevertheless.

'He would have stayed and gone to look for his father. They are fond of one another, Rupert might well have said something, man to man. I preferred not to take that risk. I regret the kind of person I was last Friday.'

Yes. Yes, Bassett said to himself.

He turned to Mr Pugh-Talbot. 'Where were you at seven when your son arrived?'

'In the garden.'

'Intentionally keeping out of sight?'

'No, matter of fact. The garden takes some getting round, as I found out. I lost track of time, was there far longer than expected. It suddenly occurred to me how long. I rushed to the yard, back way, through the wooden gate—' He stopped abruptly; his mouth closed slowly.

'In time to see Father Lambert leaving?' Bassett asked perceptively.

A brief nod. 'Preparing to leave. Shirley was in the passenger seat. I assumed it was Shirley. The driver's door was open. The priest was on his way out but he must have forgotten something, he disappeared inside again.'

'You saw him clearly?'

'No. Just a flash of a figure in black—'

'What then?'

'My talk with Shirley was obviously going to have to wait. I went for a walk along the lane. My wife had a similar idea. It was nearly eight when we got in, just beat Julian to it.'

Bassett glanced at the clock on the mantelshelf. 'I could do with a breather. Shall we take a break?'

CHAPTER 27

Should he continue? Bassett asked himself. How long were Bob and Andy likely to be?

He had ambled round to the front of the house; stood now reflecting on his talk with the Pugh-Talbots.

Mr could have done it: killed Shirley, changed out of his suit, gone back when he was supposed to be garaging his car—to bolt the access door on Shirley's side, say. Was there when the priest turned up, knocked him out, returned when he said he was in the garden; didn't see any figure in black preparing to leave—was driving the car himself.

And yet . . .

And yet their version of events had logic. Mr feeding the police only what he thought they were entitled to know; Mrs Pugh-Talbot fearing—Fearing what?

For an astute businesswoman she had been incredibly inept at sticking to her story. Those harmless white lies. She had made up her mind that Julian was to be the seven p.m. visitor; worse—that Julian had fathered the child. What other reason could there be for his visit? Julian had to be saved from himself, prevented from finding out that Shirley was pregnant . . .

Bassett's musings slowed. He began filling his pipe, and amending them. There was more to Eva's white lies than concern for her son. Like Bertie, she had sensed that something was terribly wrong. If he were honest, Bassett would have to confess that in the beginning he suspected she *knew* what was wrong. And her suspicions revolved around not only her son. That sleepless night . . . the trip to the flat at crack of dawn . . . True, Julian had turned up at seven, the appointed time, but so had Father Lambert appeared . . . also *Rupert*. Earlier than seven, granted, but what was a time? And Rupert had been quick to rush to Shirley, he'd said it was office worries that brought him home, but he *had* strayed in the past . . . Moreover, Rupert had been in and out of the house on Friday evening, and finally went off until close on eight o'clock, saying he'd gone for a walk . . . Oh yes, Eva had reason to be concerned.

Even if she had gone for a walk too, and met up with him she had reason to be concerned.

He ambled round to the door of Shirley's flat; went on to stand in the yard where Mr might have been standing when he saw the priest's car. He pictured Shirley's body being carried out—how lucky for the murderer; a few more seconds and Mr would have been a witness—and then Bassett pictured the priest . . . And it came to him in a flash, so simple, he couldn't think why he hadn't thought of it ages ago, how Father Lambert had been got into the car—by one person, not two.

One person could have done it, alone.

He thought again of Mrs Pugh-Talbot. For an astute woman . . . Innocent or guilty? Guilty, she would have made sure of her story before she opened her mouth, and stuck to it, surely. On the other hand, a *clever* woman often fares better if she pretends she's not, in business as well as in life. A double bluff?

He sighed. Could as easily apply to her husband.

Slowly, he started retracing his steps. He would still put his money on two murderers, one killed Shirley, the other Father Lambert. Freddie Palmer and—? He was about to round the corner of the house when he heard voices: Helen's and Julian's. He halted.

'You had your ear to the door! Listening to what your mum and dad were saying! How could you!' Helen accusing.

Julian entreating. 'Please, Helen. All I want to know is, are you positive it was Tommy you saw leaving the flat?'

'I'm positive.'

'You were close enough to see for certain? You didn't just assume it was Tommy?'

'For goodness' sake! It was Tommy. I ought to know Tommy when I see him. He was wearing that yellow pull-over thing Shirley knitted for him. There can't be two of *them* in the area!'

'OK. Ssh. Here's Mother—'

Bassett gave them time to move away before he walked on. Slowly. His face a blank, as if turned to stone. Inside he felt sick. Cold, empty, sick.

Rupert Pugh-Talbot was alone in the drawing-room, staring out of a window, a whisky tumbler in his hand. He turned, eyebrows going up friendly fashion, although not completely erasing his frown.

'I found what you cunningly chose to call a chat most interesting, old man.'

'Cunningly?'

'How was Shirley killed?'

'She was strangled.'

'And Father Lambert?'

'The post-mortem showed that in addition to the injury that killed him Father Lambert also received two blows to the head, one of which definitely couldn't have been self-inflicted or accidental.'

'I see. Then Uncle Bertie—?' The light had gone from the man's eyes.

'We believe the killer was driving the priest's car. It's possible the car was deliberately aimed at Bertie, to distract him. If so, the ploy had an opposite effect, for Bertie shook his fist at the driver, looked harder at him than he might otherwise have done, and by so doing retained subconsciously not a face—but the back of a neck and an impression of fair hair. The priest's hair was dark.

'While the deaths were believed to be suicide that impression lay dormant. When we began asking a new set of questions it surfaced. Bertie told me of his suspicions. It's possible he conveyed those suspicions to someone else. And so had to be quietened. I'm sorry.'

Eva Pugh-Talbot, pale, strangely beautiful, came in. 'Mr Bassett—' It was a greeting.

Her husband held out a hand. She didn't take it, but she did go and stand next to him. He placed an arm around her shoulders, seemed to give her a squeeze.

'I've been talking to Julian,' she told Bassett. 'He says he came to see you last night.'

'With Penny. She's a nice girl.'

She looked up at her husband. 'He had found Shirley new digs, that's all, Rupert. She didn't want us to know until it was finalized.'

'Why the hell didn't Julian say so!'

'We didn't exactly go out of our way to ask him, did we, dear.' To Bassett: 'I might have saved myself considerable heartache if I had put it to Julian point blank.'

'Considerable,' Bassett agreed.

'You've more questions to ask?' she said.

There had been further questions. Why didn't Mr stop when he saw Helen with Bertie? He was family, surely they wouldn't have minded him butting in for a moment? Why did he 'wrap up warm' and insist his wife did the same, as if he knew there would be a long cold search in front of them, when they went to look for Bertie? He, Bassett, would have grabbed the first coat to hand, if he'd bothered with a coat; Bertie could have suffered a heart attack, could be lying only yards from the house. And why did Mr go home to use a telephone when Tom Johnson's was nearer?

The questions now seemed superfluous; he would be asking them purely for the record. And he would receive answers. The answers would be feasible, given the kind of people they were. Vagaries of human nature . . .

His silence was misinterpreted. 'I'm in the hot seat?' Rupert Pugh-Talbot said with a frosty loss of expression. 'No alibi. Denied being here. Damn it, man, wouldn't I have fixed myself up with an alibi? Isn't that the norm? Fix yourself an alibi first?'

'It could be said that you didn't know you were going to need one,' Bassett said equably. 'That you walked into a situation on Friday evening. It could be suggested that you did what you could afterwards: had your wife forget you were home by six, had someone lined up to vouch for you at your office. You began the process by lying to the police during preliminary investigations. The office would have to wait until Monday; but by Monday the story was out, no need to jeopardize yourself. Say nothing. The story was suicide. Q.E.D.

'On the other hand—' ignoring the other's wide-eyed look of incredulity—'you might have told the truth in the first instance. Your buying petrol in Glevebourne at five-forty doesn't prove you came home; you might have been elsewhere till eight o'clock. But we are talking *murder* now. If you came home at eight, your wife is in a vulnerable position—she must have been alone in the house; and that won't do. Far better if you were here too. If you spoke to Shirley after your wife, if you saw Father Lambert come and go. Do you see? You could have cooked up this latest version of events between you.'

'My God!' Rupert Pugh-Talbot seemed about to spring. 'How dare you—'

A placatory gesture stopped him. 'I am merely pointing out how others may view it, Mr Pugh-Talbot.'

The telephone. Bob Greenaway for Bassett.

'Harry, we have a confession. Palmer. He is dead. Motorway pile-up. He left a message for his sister on her answering machine. The child was his, he killed Shirley.'

The Pugh-Talbots were trying not to show curiosity.

'That was Inspector Greenaway,' Bassett informed them. 'His regrets, he will be tied up for some time. You'll be pleased to hear, however, that Shirley's murderer—and the father of her child—has been identified.'

'Do we know him?'

'I think not. You may tell Julian. Tell him: Palmer.'

'Ready?' Andy said. The tape started running.

'Tessa, Freddie. Listen to me. Whatever I say, promise you'll listen to the end. Promise . . . I've been with police all day. I tripped up, told them there was no money from the last jobs I pulled, that K. cheated me. I thought they would get off my back, but I think I've sunk myself deeper into the mire. Tess, I can't go on, I can't hide from myself. I killed Shirley. Yes, Shirley. I'll kill again, I know I will, there's a devil in me. Tess, I'm scared . . .'

Sounds of sobbing were interrupted by a frantic, 'I haven't finished yet, keep listening.' The voice evened out. 'You should have seen how she looked at me—as if I was scum. Accused me of rape. I'd never do that, Tess . . .' A moan came next, ending in: 'No, that's a lie, let's have the truth. I used my charm. Charm!' He spat the word out. 'You see what I've become? I'd pinched something from the house, I went back and made love to Shirley . . . But I knew what I was doing, Tess!' The voice became tense, threatening. 'Never let anyone say I'm a weirdo who needs crime to get turned on. It was self-preservation, I swear . . . No excuse, is it?

'I didn't mean to kill her. Easy to say now, but it happens to be the truth. Her face. She hated me. I put a hand on her neck, she laughed, said it wouldn't do me any good. The next thing I knew she was limp. I couldn't move, I sat staring at her, covered her face with her hair, that silky hair. She was so fragile, Tess. She didn't fight me, she let me kill her . . .' Pitiful sobs . . . 'She was having my baby, I didn't know, I didn't know . . . I heard the door downstairs, fled to the next room and stood behind the door ready to run. I thought whoever it was would go into the bedroom and I'd make my escape. It never entered my head they'd look for her. He did, he called her name, started to come into the room where I was. I thought I'd had it. I lashed out. Knocked him out. Hit him, Tess, hit a priest. I didn't kill him, I swear. I never meant to hurt anyone, I never meant to hurt my sweet Shirley, believe that, please, and forgive me . . . Tess, I'm nearly out of coins—'

'Listen to this,' Bob Greenaway said.

'—Love me a little. Scrub this now. My insurance policy is yours but my death has to be an accident, there won't be a penny for suicide. Love me, Tess . . .'

Bob switched it off. 'His sister didn't destroy it. She wanted us to know he wasn't all bad, he was sorry for what he had done. A cheat to the end, though.'

'The irony of it is,' said Andy, 'his death was an accident in the end, recorded on police video. An articulated lorry jackknifed in front of him, he couldn't have avoided it if he'd tried.'

'Where do we go from here?' Bob said wearily. 'Who did kill the priest and Uncle Bertie? And why?'

Bassett told him. 'Trouble is—we have to prove it. Anything from Forensics yet on the hat?'

Andy went to see. Bob Greenaway went to organize a warrant. Bassett got on the phone to Briony House.

CHAPTER 28

Bassett drew up outside Helen's bungalow, Bob Greenaway and Andy Miller went on to Tom Johnson's place. The Pugh-Talbots would have made sure they would both be at home.

Helen was in her back garden, a solitary figure rising from a vast cushion of dahlias, colourful even under a sky growing grey with storm clouds. Bassett watched her bend to sniff one bloom, cup another in both hands and sink her face into its petals. He walked towards her. She saw him, let him come, only moving to meet him when a spitting cat leapt out from behind an outbuilding, halting Bassett in his tracks.

She shoohed the cat away. 'She's not usually fierce. She's got kittens in the shed. She's being a good mother.'

Bassett made a humorous face. 'May we talk?'

'Inside?' The back door opened on to the same room Bassett had been in the previous night. 'Come through to the other room, it's tidier.'

'Here will do admirably.' He drew Helen a chair. 'Sit down, Helen.' He sat opposite.

'What have I done?' she said playfully, yet warily.

Bassett said with mock severity, 'You fibbed when you told me Shirley had named Julian as the baby's father. She said no such thing. You plucked Julian out of his mother's conversation with Shirley, noted the emphasis, and took it a stage further. You also fibbed about Shirley saying: He would lose everything . . .' His eyes appeared to crinkle at the corners. 'No irreparable harm done, fortunately.'

He opened his notebook, pretended to scan the pages.

'Last Friday you answered the phone . . . heard a car . . . and so went home. Mm. After you had gone our murderer arrived on foot, was there when Father Lambert arrived. We tried to figure out what might have followed.'

He looked up. 'Do you want to hear this?'

'Yes.' And a polite please.

'We thought the killer, having strangled Shirley, was then caught, trapped, in the flat. In order to escape he knocked Father Lambert out. But daren't let him go for fear Father Lambert had recognized him. What should he do?'

'We know what he did.'

'Carried them both out to the car, yes. Must have had help, we thought. Given the priest's build, the fact that he was unconscious—which he must have been or else he'd have protested, to say the least—it would have been very difficult for just one person, single-handed, to have got him into that car.

'However, there is a way it could have been done by one person only . . .' He gave Helen a direct look.

She seemed breathless and a little afraid.

'Now to Uncle Bertie, who shook his fist at the driver when the car nearly ran him down—and saw what remained in his memory as fair hair at the nape of the driver's neck.

'I was with Bertie, as you know, before he met you on the path to the lake. His suspicions that someone else, not the priest, had been driving the car, were preying on his mind. He mentioned Tom. I think he was sounding me out—what did I know? Probing, trying to find out—'

'Not Tom,' Helen put in. 'It couldn't have been Tom.'

'You are very fond of Tom, aren't you? You're in love with him. Always have been.'

She nodded dumbly.

'You would lie for him. Would do anything to protect him, keep him safe.'

'If I could. If he'd done anything. But he didn't.'

'Last Friday, after you had heard Tom, and Mrs Pugh-Talbot talking to Shirley, after you had come home—you saw Tom climbing the stile leading to a short cut to the big house. You were naturally curious. He used his short cut—you cycled there, and took up a watching position in the tackle shed—

'How could I? I had my other job to go to.'

'Your job at the Pig and Whistle is not—how shall I put it?—imperative. You don't go because you need money, you go more for the company. You aren't compelled to turn up on time, although you usually do; no one is waiting for you to take over so that they can go off duty. You are a welcome pair of hands, but—'

Helen half laughed. 'Who told you this? Maisie? It was Maisie, wasn't it? Wait till I see her!'

'You turned up on Friday, but an hour late—'

'She's lying! Just because she didn't see much of me—'

'Is the young reporter also lying?' Bassett said. 'He frequents the Pig and Whistle, does he not? You hadn't been over-friendly with him until last Friday, when you had a chat with him about a manmade lake. Some creative writing, a few photos, including one of the parched area farther on, you said, and he could have a good local interest story. All grist to the mill. Might have his editor applauding his initiative—'

'You're not going to say I knew when those women would find—what they found! That's ridiculous!'

'You couldn't have foreseen that, no. But you know your area, as I know mine. A Saturday in September, most folks' holidays over—you could be fairly confident that no one would be picnicking much before early afternoon. In any event, a car and a man and woman lying on the ground—people would be inclined to keep at a distance.

'Anyhow, you had all possibilities covered. If the bodies hadn't already been discovered you would have taken the youth by a circuitous route, making sure you touched on the picnic area, and you two would have come upon them. If they had already been found you would have taken him to the spot, and would have contrived anyway to furnish him with his scoop. One way or another you would attract attention away from Tom Johnson. How better than by linking Shirley with Father Lambert? You guessed the lad would be receptive, in the wake of recent disclosures about a certain Catholic Bishop. I imagine that was what first gave you the idea—'

'Mr Bassett, I could sue you for slander.'

'Hardly, my dear, we are alone, you and I.'

He got up. Did Helen think he was going to go? She

watched him absent-mindedly open and close a cupboard door; and another, before turning to her again.

'Last Friday you spotted Tom returning, you thought, to Shirley's flat. You went to your hole in the wall to watch for him. Then you would have gone to eavesdrop again. Tom didn't go to the flat, he went to fetch his cigarettes from the garden shed. You weren't to know that, of course. You watched, no sign of him, decided you must have missed him, and so trotted across . . .'

Unseen. Mr fiddling with fairy lights.

'Tom didn't kill Shirley,' Helen said with something like a small laugh. 'Haven't you heard? The police have a confession! Tommy didn't do it!'

'But you *thought* he had,' Bassett said.

'No-o.' She shook her head, as a fond mother might do to a child who is making up stories.

'You trotted across and found Shirley dead in bed, Father Lambert unconscious in another room. And you thought Tommy had done it.'

'No-o.' Still the fond mother to her child.

'He had to be saved. You had to save him. I can't be certain how your mind worked then, but you're a strong and healthy woman, perhaps you decided that Shirley should be found in the woods, victim of a passer-through, heaven knows we hear of such victims daily. You could carry her out to her car, drive her there. Ah, but what about the priest?

'You know better than I what decided you to use his car and arrange the deaths as you did. Maybe it came to you while you were putting Shirley's coat on her.

'You then stole downstairs, opened the door a crack, perhaps heard Julian's sports car, witnessed his encounter with his mother—which would later reinforce the notion you had that he was involved somehow—saw him turn his car and depart. No reason for his mother to be wandering about after that. Access door bolted. Way clear. With the strength of desperation you carried Shirley down and into the car. Father Lambert's car.

'You didn't have to carry Father Lambert down. At each stage of the proceedings you gained in confidence. If anyone found Shirley now—you had found her like that in the car, had gone in, heard sounds, bashed the intruder—too late you realized it was Father Lambert . . . When Father Lambert started to come round, disorientated, groggy, you adjusted the prepared explanations. Father! Are you all right? There's been an intruder, I'm taking Shirley to the hospital, you must come too! Take off your cassock, don't want you tripping on it and tumbling downstairs! . . . There, into the back seat, lie down, don't want you passing out . . .

'Or was that when you struck him again? Did he begin to regain his wits, leaned forward to speak to Shirley, to touch her, saw to his horror that she was dead? You would have had to hit him then, wouldn't you, to keep him quiet?

'You put his cassock on. He wouldn't have worn a hat to visit Shirley, but it was there in the car. You piled your hair on top of your head, plonked the hat on to hold it in place. Uncle Bertie didn't see fair hair, he saw an expanse of white neck. A young woman's neck is altogether different from a man's. *This* was the image Bertie tried to get clear in his memory.'

'No-o-o.'

'You did have one small fright. When Mr Pugh-Talbot appeared in the yard as you were about to leave the flat for the last time. Sight of him—he shouldn't have been home yet—unnerved you. You might not have been so venturesome if you had known, he could have caught you! Your fright put you so on edge your driving was downright dangerous.'

He paused, opened and shut, still apparently absent-mindedly, another cupboard door. When he turned to Helen she smiled. A different smile.

'This is getting silly,' she said.

'We all do silly things, Helen, including you. It was silly of you to lie about Bertie sitting on a log to finish his smoke. Why did you? Because telling me about the lake would have been tantamount to admitting you knew exactly how to find him when you went back with a spade? Better to have said nothing. It was common knowledge that Bertie liked to sit and contemplate the water. As he did yesterday—the butt of the selfsame cigar he lit when he was with me was found by the lakeside.'

Bassett had worked his way round to the door he had seen Helen go to the previous night. He opened it. Not a pantry as he had supposed: a broom cupboard. On the floor, a thick newspaper. On the newspaper, a long narrow dent as would be left by a spade standing there . . . Minute specks, and staining: to experienced eyes, blood.

He shut the door with the same absence of comment as with the other cupboard doors.

'You were right yesterday when you suggested Mr Pugh-Talbot had probably gone full circle to Briony House. You knew he had, you were on the lookout for him as you pedalled to Tom's for a spade—quicker than fetching your own—raced with it to the lakeside, and back again. Back here. You had to bring the spade home to clean it, no makeshift cleaning would suffice, Tom keeps his tools in tip-top condition.

'But you couldn't clean it straight away, your friends, you dared not be late for them, their shopping excursion was the highlight of their week. If you were noticeably late they might chatter about it, in the shops, elsewhere. Nor would Tom miss the spade for one night. You knew he would be working on plans for Mrs Blest's pergola. So the spade rested in this cupboard.

'You were going to return it after dark last night—until you got to the rear of the house and saw that we were in the kitchen, whose lights might have given you away. You had expected Tom and his guest to be behind the french windows, whose lights fell on another part of the garden.

'You retreated, holding the spade in front of you when you heard the door go. I fancy it slid from your grasp once, your torch too. Torch light shining for a second on the hem of your skirt told me who you were. You finally returned the spade after I left you. I saw you.'

She was staring at him with a kind of wonderment. 'Was that where I slipped up?'

'No. You could have been helping Tom out of a jam. You slipped up this morning. I heard Julian ask if you were positive it was Tom you saw leaving the flat. You said you were—and you described a yellow garment Tom was wearing.'

'Yes . . . Yes, I did, didn't I?' She shrugged: the sort of shrug you might give when you've made a mistake but not a dreadful one. 'Silly again.'

''Fraid so. Tom wasn't wearing the yellow when he went to see Shirley; he was wearing it when he went back for his cigarettes. And you were adamant that you had seen nobody, you were feeling too miserable, etcetera, etcetera.'

'Yes . . .' Slowly her face lit up. 'I did tell you, didn't I? I've been telling you all along Tommy didn't do it. I knew you'd believe me sometime!'

CHAPTER 29

'A dreadful thing, obsession,' Father Fitzroy's housekeeper said. 'Tom Johnson would never have married her, you say.'

'No,' Bassett said. 'He never pretended he would.'

'Was she too isolated, do you think?'

'Who knows, Mrs Pomfrey? It's possible. I really don't know. But she certainly had a dangerous fixation. She told us how for years she had conjured up reasons for Tom's not asking her to be his. First, she was an only child; it would have been selfish of him to take her away from her parents. When her father died—ditto her mother, who now depended on her for everything. After her mother passed away—a suitable period of mourning had to be observed. Then, just when the time seemed right, along came Shirley, capturing everybody's heart including Tom's.

'She became insanely jealous of Shirley's friendship with Tom, till in the end every innocent meeting was seen as an assignation, every look and word held hidden meaning. She imagined a secret love-affair, and so on. The fact that there *was* a secret affair, though not with Tom, didn't help matters.'

'But she must have known deep down there was nothing going on. Else why did she run telling tales to Tom about the baby?'

'In her eyes Tommy was so perfect the baby couldn't be his, she decided; he was being made a fool of by Shirley the harlot. If she could get that across to him she might get him back, he was bound to turn to her for comfort.'

'And alas, it backfired on her.'

'Alas, it backfired, Mrs Pomfrey. When she heard Tommy declare his love for Shirley, ask her to be his wife, she knew it was the end for her, she would never have him. Yet she still so loved the man she twice killed in order, she thought, to protect him.'

'One would have thought she would hate him.'

'No, on the contrary,' Bassett said. 'She told us how it gave her a feeling of fulfilment. She looked upon it as sacrificing herself for the man she loved.'

'Oh dear,' Mrs Pomfrey said uncomfortably.

'The supreme sacrifice,' Bassett said. 'Had she been caught she would have confessed to Shirley's murder too; her story would have to be believed, Tommy's never, even if he owned up.'

'Which he wouldn't have done, being innocent.' Father Fitzroy spoke at last. Tersely.

Mrs Pomfrey looked at him. 'Her mind must have gone, poor soul.' Father Fitzroy glared. He was without pity.

Bassett said: 'It certainly went towards the end, Mrs Pomfrey. Bertie had always been a good friend to her. She told us she had to brainwash herself before she could strike him down. In fact she adored the old gentleman . . . Until Bertie's death she hardly put a foot wrong. Made mischief, told lies, but none we would have been able to prove, alas.' Impossible to prove, for instance, that Julian *hadn't* been a regular clandestine visitor to Shirley's flat, or that the girl *hadn't* told Helen the things Helen said she had. 'After Bertie's death—well, confusion set in. She said too much, and she grew careless.'

'Indeed! And did she show no remorse for striking down a priest!' Father Fitzroy barked.

Bassett shook his head sadly. 'It wasn't a priest she struck down, Father. It doesn't lessen the gravity of her crime, I know—but for months she had imagined Tom to be Shirley's secret boyfriend; then came the pregnancy. She told us Julian was responsible, a lie, one of many designed to throw us off the scent. She never knew the true identity of the boyfriend, she had merely convinced herself it was Tom. When she saw Father Lambert lying in one room, Shirley's body in another, *then*, she said, the real truth dawned on her. All the time Shirley had been claiming the boyfriend was abroad he was in fact here—Father Lambert. As far as she was concerned, Father Lambert had forfeited the right to any respect befitting a priest. When she struck him down he was, to her, just an ordinary, sinful man.'

'Oh dear,' Mrs Pomfrey murmured again.

Bassett's hand went to an inside pocket. 'Shirley left a letter. It was to have been posted to Father Lambert if she had kept an appointment she made with a clinic in London. I thought you might like to have a copy, Father, in case the Church was left with any doubt.'

Father Fitzroy's hands trembled slightly as he took the sheet of paper and unfolded it. He read; after a while looked up. 'It's all here, the whole story.'

'The whole story, the reasons why she had booked into the clinic. Most importantly it makes it quite clear that Father Lambert was entirely blameless,' Bassett said kindly, holding the elderly priest's gaze.

'Indeed and it does,' the other said quietly, the Irish coming out. He read the letter once more, pausing when he came to the end. 'She was still a child herself,' he said; and he read the last lines aloud: '"*I hope you will pray for me. Please Father, forgive me. Love, Shirley.*"'

He gave the letter to Mrs Pomfrey to read, went and stood looking out of the window while she did so.

At length he turned. 'I too have a confession to make. I *did* wonder about those visits of Shirley's—and Father Lambert's reticence. He was—fond of her. And he was a radical—' His eyes met Bassett's.

Bassett's eyes said: I know.

'Shirley *could* have been going away to avoid a scandal, Father Lambert could have gone on Friday evening to make a last ditch attempt to keep her here, and the two of them would face the music. Their deaths could have been brought about by a fanatic who saw them together—'

'But now we know what really did happen,' Mrs Pomfrey cut in cheerfully. 'Now,' she said, jumping to her feet, 'I don't know about you, Father, Mr Bassett—but I could do with another cup of tea!'

Never had a case affected him so deeply, Bassett thought as he drove towards Oakleigh and home. Although every case had at the time it was going on.

In his mind's eye he saw again Father Fitzroy's face after he had read Shirley's letter. He pictured Shirley and Father Lambert as they might have been when alive. He saw Uncle Bertie's grin, the humour behind Bertie's 'Olé!' And he saw eyes that shone, albeit insanely, for love of a man.

He was a little disappointed that Julian had deemed it necessary to eavesdrop when he was talking to his parents; he had given his word. But then, if he hadn't indulged in some eavesdropping himself he wouldn't have overheard that young man's conversation with Helen . . .

He drew up outside his widowed neighbour's house. She was leaving today, he was here to collect his dog and give her the biggest hug . . .

He gave Grace a pot plant to take with her. 'And you had better have this,' she said. She held up an object—a stuffed fabric draught-excluder for the bottom of a door, shaped like an elongated Dachshund. 'I won't need it where I'm going. And your dog has been going steady with it for the past fortnight.'

Bassett grinned, then laughed, then he looked heavenwards. 'Oh, Mary!' he chuckled.

Life was back to normal.